W9-BLC-890

STORIES ABOUT MONSTERS . . .
STORIES ABOUT MURDERS . . .
STORIES ABOUT MADMEN . . .

America's grand master of the macabre chooses a shroudful of his fearful favorites. Stories by such world-renowned goosebump-inducers like Sir Arthur Conan Doyle, Clark Ashton Smith, William Hodgson, Ambrose Bierce and . . . . Gahan Wilson.

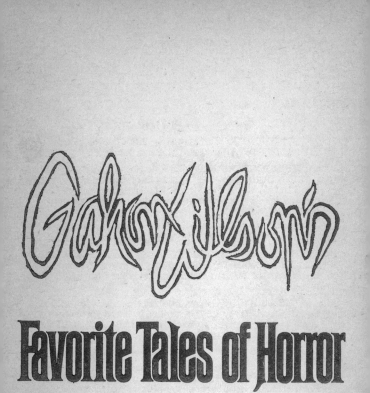

Gahan Wilson

Favorite Tales of Horror

collected by
Gahan Wilson

tempo books

GROSSET & DUNLAP
A FILMWAYS COMPANY
PUBLISHERS • NEW YORK

ACKNOWLEDGMENTS

KITTY FISHER, copyright Charles Birkin from his collection MY NAME IS DEATH published by Award Books

THE STONE SHIP by William Hope Hodgson
THE TRADER OF THE DUST by Clark Ashton Smith
LUELLA MILLER by Mary Wilkins Freeman
Reprinted by permission of Arkham House Publishers, Inc., Sauk City, Wisconsin

RATS by M.R. James from COLLECTED GHOST STORIES, copyright Edward Arnold Publishers Ltd. Reprinted by permission

HORROR OF THE HEIGHTS by Sir Arthur Conan Doyle from THE CONAN DOYLE STORIES, copyright Baskervilles Investments and Jonathan Cape/John Murray Publishers Ltd. Reprinted by permission

THE CLOCK by William Fryer Harvey. Published in the United States in 1928 by E.P. Dutton & Co., Inc., and reprinted with their permission. Published in Great Britain by J.M. Dent & Sons, Ltd.

THE SEA WAS WET AS WET COULD BE by Gahan Wilson. Originally appeared in "Playboy Magazine"; copyright © 1967 by Playboy.

THE IDOL WITH HANDS OF CLAY by Sir Frederick Treves. Copyright and reprinted by permission of Cassell and Company Ltd.

THE HARBOR MASTER by Robert W. Chambers from THE KING IN YELLOW AND OTHER TALES OF SUPERNATURAL HORROR by Robert W. Chambers, Dover Publications Inc.

Copyright © 1976 by Gahan Wilson
All rights reserved
Published Simultaneously in Canada
ISBN: 0-448-12627-3 (Tempo Edition)
      0-448-13523-X (Library Edition)
Library of Congress Catalog Card No. 76-47890
A Tempo Books Original
Printed in the United States of America

Contents

GENERAL INTRODUCTION *Gahan Wilson* 1

KITTY FISHER *Charles Birkin* 3

THE TREADER OF THE DUST *Clark Ashton Smith* 21

THE HORROR OF THE HEIGHTS *Sir Arthur Conan Doyle* 33

THE STONE SHIP *William Hope Hodgson* 53

THE SEA WAS WET AS WET COULD BE *Gahan Wilson* 87

LUELLA MILLER *Mary Wilkins Freeman* 103

THE IDOL WITH HANDS OF CLAY *Sir Frederick Treves* 121

MY FAVORITE MURDER *Ambrose Bierce* 131

THE CLOCK *William Fryer Harvey* 143

THE HARBOR-MASTER *Robert W. Chambers* 151

RATS *M.R. James* 179

General Introduction

ALL OF THESE STORIES have, appropriately enough, haunted me. Having read them I cannot get rid of them; they will not let me be.

Sometimes I'll manage to forget them entirely for long periods of time, but this gives me no feeling of confidence for I know only too well they lurk hidden in their permanent niches in my subconscious. At the sight of a doll's head lolling oddly on its shoulders, I will instantly recall that awful moment in *Kitty Fisher*, which I won't describe lest I reduce its ghastly impact when you come across it for yourself, and once again experience that old familiar shudder.

Stories that stay with you, as these have with me, permanently affect your environment. An empty house, no matter how pleasant and matter of fact, just won't be the same once you've read *The Clock*, and

1

any garbage dump glimpsed from your car will seem even more sinister after you've read *Rats*. Vampires, on the other hand, look considerable more human to anyone who has met *Luella Miller,* and no one who has encountered the pathetic wretch in *The Idol with Hands of Clay* will ever be quite so intimidated by the medical profession as they might have been before.

These stories are, first of all, remarkably entertaining. Their authors will probably give you a few new insights into your own complexity. Then you are sure to have a number of stimulating frights, not to mention and occasional, and very probably nervous, chuckle. I consider it a privilege to have this chance to introduce them to you and your psyche.

Kitty Fisher

Charles Birkin

The sense of steady, swelling doom you get as you read this story of really nice people working in concert to destroy their really nice lives is quite remarkable, and it features as pathetic and heartbreaking a villain as I've ever come across.

ALERIE QUINN was subjecting her husband to a critical inspection, which was quite out of character. "You look old-fashioned," she remarked dispassionately. "It's high time that you invested in a modern dinner jacket."

"I look old-world," Basil corrected her, "and glad of it. Would you like me to be mistaken for a pop singer?"

"Old-fashioned," Valerie insisted. "No one wears butterfly bows any more. They went out with Fred Astaire."

"I like them," said Basil, "and I like Fred Astaire. I'm the faithful type; and anyway you're always harping on about how you never notice what men wear. It's a form of perverted pride."

"I don't harp," Valerie told him pleasantly.

"Oh yes you do, my love," Basil said. "You could be the chief performer in an eisteddfod! If you really put your mind to it you could be a one-woman show, a musical Joyce Grenfell!" He pulled the butt end of his carnation through his buttonhole. "We'd better be on our way."

4

"We needn't leave for another five minutes," objected Valerie.

From long experience Basil did not argue, but took his watch from his pocket and stood staring at it pointedly. "If you are determined to be late . . ." he said.

"And a waistcoat is so dating," continued his wife, paying no attention. "Other men have graduated to cummerbunds. Why can't you?"

"Because," Basil said amiably, "I find that waistcoats are warm, conservative and useful garments. I keep necessary things in their pockets. Oh hello, Hubert!" He broke off the subject of his sartorial shortcomings as his son came into the room. "We're just going. As you know, we're leaving the children in your capable hands."

Hubert smiled. "Have fun!" he said. He was a tall boy of eighteen, fair-haired and loose-limbed. It was already obvious that when he reached maturity and had filled out he would be strikingly good-looking. He wore an open-necked shirt and black jeans, the uniform of his generation.

"I'm sorry I had to ask you to put off your date," his father apologized, "but this evening could be quite important to us."

"I know," said Hubert. "It doesn't matter a bit. You're not unique. Nobody," he allowed magnanimously, "can get baby sitters these days."

"What had you planned to do?" inquired Valerie.

Hubert gave a shrug. "Some of us were going to Martha Lucas's. Nothing special. Records—and that sort of thing. She lives on the river at Chiswick. I can go there another night equally well."

The corners of Valerie's mouth crinkled. "You're a sensible and agreeable young man," she told him appreciatively, "and the Lord will reward you, even if we don't!"

She went out into the night nursery and they could hear her talking to Kate who, under protest, was already in bed. She shared the room with Lucy, the baby. "Good night, Kitty," Valerie was saying. "Now be a co-operative pet-pie and try to go to sleep, and for pity's sake don't wake up

Lucy. We won't be all that late, one o'clock at the outside. I'll be back before then in all probability, but your father might have to stay on for the celebrations." There came the murmur of Kate's answering voice, followed by her mother's valediction: "Good night, Kitty darling." After a pause she added more softly: " 'Night 'night, 'Lucy Locket'." When Valerie came back she was holding Kate's supper tray on which rested a plate speckled with biscuit crumbs and a tumbler rimmed and discoloured by smears of milk. She took it out into the kitchen.

Valerie had made no real effort to cling on to youth. Her charm did not depend on being that of springtime. Her brown hair was streaked with grey, and her large intelligent eyes sparkled with humour. It was to charm more than to beauty that she owed her potent attraction, although when an occasion demanded it she could give the illusion of great beauty. Her russet dress, admittedly expensive, was simple and well cut and suited to her years, and her jewelry consisted of one wide gold bracelet.

She was accompanying Basil to the opening of a thriller, *The Even Tide,* at the King's Theatre. Actually they were to be the guests of Alex and Audrey Wardell, whose daughter, Zandra, was playing her first part in the West End; and afterwards they had all been invited to go on to a party at The White Elephant.

Basil was an actor by profession. He was not a big star in the accepted sense, but nearly always he was in work. He was experienced and reliable and sufficiently versatile, and over the years he had built up a faithful following, especially among the ranks of the munching ladies at matinées, who admired loyally his crooked smile and gentlemanly demeanour. At regular intervals he took over leading rôles when other, and perhaps more dynamic actors, left the casts of long-running plays. He had begun, also, to appear with flattering regularity on television, which was an additional and welcome source of income.

Valerie, too, had been on the stage. Being the possessor of a fey, unusual quality, she had achieved success almost from the start, but after marriage had not pressed on with her career to the best of her potential since she had decided that her family was of more importance, but she still appeared occasionally whenever she was offered a part in a play which interested her, and when it was urged sincerely that it was one that only she could play.

Hubert was shaping well at R.A.D.A., and their hopes for his future looked justified. Basil and Valerie Quinn were delighted with their children. After Hubert's birth there had been a second son, Jock, who had died in infancy, which had been an intolerable sadness, and a gap of nine years had elapsed before Kate had made her appearance, to be joined after a lapse of a further five by Lucy, who was now thirteen months old.

Basil was, for some obscure reason, determined that Lucy had outstanding musical talent and was destined to be an opera singer. The pet name bestowed on her, "Lucy Locket", was a natural, and he was apt to refer to his baby's throat as her "pocket", from whose golden velvet depths untold wealth would one day flow. "Lucy," he would confide facetiously to anyone who was prepared to listen to him, "is our insurance policy against the blighting blast of penurious old age when nobody will any longer employ us. Hubert will naturally have his own wife and family to support and care for and Kitty—I am already conditioning her to the notion, so that she will be secure—will marry a rich and kind and clever man and be his pampered pet. It is 'Lucy Locket' who will provide us with the comforts that will surely be our right in the winter of our lives. Wait and see. She will be the loveliest soprano of them all!" The recipients of this inordinate boasting would smile at him indulgently.

Kate was a completely different type from the extrovert Hubert. She was a composed, self-sufficient little girl, shy and somewhat secretive. She was attracted to all domesticated pursuits, sewing, painting her dolls, and playing the piano, at which she had begun to show a considerable aptitude. At times Valerie found her difficult to understand, but Basil adored her, as he did all of his offspring, and declared that her determination and force of character would make its mark in grown-up life, although not necessarily in the world of drama.

Valerie refrained from telling him that beneath the child's serene demeanor there was concealed not only strength but an obstinate will of iron, and a jealous possessiveness that she thought frightening. She tried to reassure herself that Kate would eventually grow out of these failings to her make-up. The middle one of three children, in order to survive as an individual, was often forced into asserting itself, sometimes by aggression, sometimes, as in Kate's case, passively. The problem was not easy of solution and Valerie was filled with unease.

All their friends were vastly amused by Kate. She was enchanting with her dark burnished hair and spontaneous and unexpectedly bewitching smile; always demure in the vaguely Alice-in-Wonderland clothes in which she was dressed.

Alex Wardell was one of Kate's godfathers and he thought her fascinating. On her fifth birthday he had presented her with an enormous doll in the form of a Zulu warrior, splendidly bedecked in beads and anklets and feathers and nearly five feet in height, bearing a shield and assagai. "She must get used early in life to the idea of having a man in her bed," he had said to Basil laughingly, "even if in this brave new world it should be miscegenation!" Kate had been ecstatic over the gift. She had never imagined such a gorgeous present, and had christened it "Othello".

When Valerie had collected her from the kindergarten at the end of her first term, Miss Harley, the headmistress, had praised her progress wholeheartedly. They had been standing together at the foot of the steps outside the school, waiting for the pupils to emerge. "A most intelligent little person," Miss Harley had said. "She has the staff in fits! There is one thing, though, that I think it is my duty to tell you, Mrs. Quinn." Miss Harley had bestowed on her a quick professional smile, her spectacles glinting in the pale March sunshine, before she had delivered her blow. "Never," she had said, "never in all my long experience have I known a child of Kate's age, or indeed of any age, to be so utterly aloof. She has no contact, and wishes to make none, with her contemporaries. Out of the classroom she chooses to live in a world of her own, where no one can touch her."

At the time Valerie had gazed at her blankly and had been nettled by what she considered to be needless and rather nebulous criticism, but she had not liked hearing her own largely unadmitted fears put so firmly into words.

The party at The White Elephant could be very useful to Basil. Audrey Wardell had told her Humphrey Brecknock would be present and that shortly he would be casting Beverly Bryant's new play in which the male lead might have been tailored for Basil. It was an adaptation of *No Helping Hand,* a novel which she had read and enjoyed. The two men did not know one another personally, and while Humphrey, through the nature of his job, was familiar with Basil's work, there would be no harm, as Audrey suggested, in jogging his memory by bringing them together at such a strategic moment. It had been arranged that they were to meet the Wardells in the foyer of the theatre.

Valerie came back to the drawing-room. She had on her short sable jacket. "Ready?" she asked brightly, as if Basil had been the one who had been loitering. "We mustn't be late and you're bound to take hours finding a parking place." She called out a final and muted good night through the nursery door. "Thank you, Hubert," she said again. "Your dinner is all ready in the oven. All you have to do is to take it out when you are hungry." She looked up into her husband's face. "Come along, darling."

When they had gone Hubert crossed to the long window that gave on to the Square, where the trees were beginning to bronze. Presently he saw his parents, foreshortened from where he was standing, come out and cross the pavement and get into the Jaguar. He noticed with a twinge of compassion, knowing how much he would have minded, that his father's hair was thinning. Their gleaming car made his own second-hand Austin seem very antiquated. Nevertheless he loved it. He had been given it at Christmas after he had passed his driving test, and he cherished it with a fierce pride and passion. He swung away from the window, his hands thrust into the pockets of his skin-tight jeans. He wanted to go to the Lucases' but realized without rancor that occasionally other people's plans had also to be considered. He had wished to be at Martha's tonight because Hermione Harrison had been asked, and Miss Harrison at present occupied a large part of his thoughts. She was capable of being interested in a chap, which was more than he could say of that brash bunch of conceited girls at R.A.D.A., like Judy Brent, who seemed to be interested only in themselves.

He wondered how he would spend the evening. He had lines for the next day that could be gone over, but he was a quick study and had already memorized them until he was word perfect. It was as yet too soon to think of eating. He decided to turn on the television and get himself a bottle of Coke from the refrigerator. He had just finished drinking this, and was reading the headlines in the evening paper, when the telephone rang.

It was, to his pleased surprise, Hermione Harrison. Hermione, it transpired, had been basely let down, which he could not help thinking, would for her have been a novel experience. She had arranged to drive to Martha's with Maggie Lloyd and her brother but unfortunately, and through absolutely no fault of her own, she had been delayed and they had not waited for her. Was that not, she complained, typical of Maggie? Was Hubert by any lucky chance going to Chiswick, and if so could she cadge a lift. She was quite confident of his answer, for she was not unaware of the allure she held for Hubert, so that she was none too pleased when he had to tell her that for family reasons he could not make it. She listened to his stammered explanations in an ominous silence.

"I see," she said coldly when he had finished. In answer to his question as to the feasibility of their fixing a future meeting she was evasive. "I really can't tell you, Hubert. This week and next are booked solid. You know how it is!" She did not have to underline her point that she was in brisk demand for he was fully cognizant of it. "Well, good-bye," she said. "It would have been nice if you could have seen your way to taking me, but of course I realize that you can't. It would only have been as far as Martha's. Once there I'll have no trouble at all in getting back," she added bitchily.

Hermione had succeeded in making him feel callow and a bit of a fool. Why had it been tonight that she had seen fit to ask him to do her a favor? "Wait a minute," said Hubert. "Hold on." Hermione had said that she was speaking from Bowley Crescent, which was round the corner. He could pick her up, drive her to the Lucases' and be home again in under the hour. It was still early and the kids would be safe enough for that brief time. He was sure if he had consulted them that his parents would not have objected to his making such a hasty sortie; and if he were to drive Hermione at what she now knew was inconvenience to himself, then she would be under an obligation to him and he could arrange another and more leisurely date. "I'll manage it," he said. "Be with you in a few minutes."

He put down the receiver before she could answer, and ran into the bathroom to brush his hair with Basil's monogrammed ivory brushes. Putting his head round the door into the night nursery he said in a penetrating whisper: "Kitty!"

"Yes?" He heard the rustle of the sheets as the little girl sat up in bed. He had known that at the age of nearly seven she would not be asleep. Even when he returned she would in all probability be wide awake.

"Ssh . . . !" he said warmingly. "Don't disturb Lucy or

there'll be hell to pay. Listen, Kitty. I've got to go out. I promise you I'll be back before it's properly dark. Be a poppet while I'm gone—and don't," he cautioned her, "say anything about it to anybody. Let it be our secret."

"Where are you going?" Kate whispered back, intrigued by this unexpected development.

"Not far," said Hubert reassuringly. "I told Hermione Harrison I'd drop her at Martha's. She's got no other means of getting there and I don't want to let her down."

"Oh!" said Kate. "Who's Hermione Harrison?" She sounded disapproving. She welcomed Hubert's male friends but was wary of her beloved brother's girls. There was that horrible Judy somebody who had always ignored her when she had visited the house. "Oh . . ." she said once more. "Oh, all right." She snuggled down among the pillows and after a moment heard the discreet click of the lock on the front door as Hubert closed it carefully behind him.

Kate was woken by the shrilling of the telephone. It seemed to go on and on. Why didn't Hubert answer it? Perhaps he was still with that Hermione girl. Kate climbed out of bed and pattered out into the hall. The clock on the wall showed that it was a quarter to ten, and Hubert had left at twenty past seven, or thereabouts. Why hadn't he come home? She lifted the receiver. "Hello?" she said cautiously.

"Hello?" It was Hubert's voice. "That you, Kitty? Sorry to stir you up. Wanted to check that everything was O.K. Not that there's any reason why it shouldn't be! Look, I'm speaking from a garage. Had a puncture and I've got no spare tire. Like an ass I forgot to call for it this morning. Shouldn't be too long now. Go back to bed. No need to worry."

"I'm not," said Kate with dignity.

"That's my duckling!" Hubert hung up. What he had omitted to tell her was that he had been involved in a minor collision and that a rear mudguard was in the process

of being straightened out for him as a favor by an oblig-
ing mechanic, and that it might be an hour before he
reached home. He did not want his father to discover that
he had had even a bump when he should not have been
out on the road at all, for he had given his word and felt
distinctly guilty.

Kate was not at all sleepy. It was fun being left alone
and in charge of the flat. Lucy did not count. Lucy was
only a baby. Kate contemplated staying up for a while,
maybe, if he was not too long, until Hubert came in. She
would go into the play room and have a game. She would
play at Theatres. She had been taken to one during the
New Year, when they had gone to see *Cinderella*.

She switched on the light. The room looked oddly
deserted and unfamiliar, with the toys all put away and
with the black rectangle of the window looming up at her.
She went across and drew the windmill-patterned curtains
to shut out the night. That was more cosy! Kate opened
the toy cupboard and started to pull out her assemblage
of dolls and animals. She left them in a heap and pushed
the scrubbed deal table up against the wall. Its surface
was mottled by the stains of past artistic endeavors,
some of which dated back to the time when Hubert had
been the sole occupant. She was dissatisfied with the
harsh overhead bulb. She moved the reading lamp into
the middle of the table and hung a duster over the shade.
It was the one she used for wiping off the blackboard, and
a fine mist of chalk rubbings drifted down from it as she
twitched it into position. She turned off the switch by the
door. Now there was not enough light, but it was better
and would have to do.

The table must be the stage. Caroline, her flaxen-haired
favorite, was the obvious choice for Cinderella. Joe, the
multicolored Harlequin, should be Prince Charming, and
a battered Tyrolean madchen and a down-at-heel Pier-
rette would do for the Ugly Sisters. The Fairy Queen,
from last year's tree, must of course play her own rôle.

The remainder of the toys, both human and animal, she would arrange in rows as the enthusiastic audience.

She was busying herself with this task when Lucy started to cry. Kate frowned in annoyance. Lucy was spoiled. She ruined everything always. She was a little nuisance. Kate knew that unless she was picked up she would go on crying. Well, there was nothing else for it, she would have to bring her in here, and then she might stop. If she were left alone she would bawl her head off. "Lucy Locket" indeed! It was a silly name, but Daddy could be silly where Lucy was concerned, and so could Mummy. Kate put a pink frog among the second row of spectators, sliding it in between a flop-eared Dalmatian and an anemic grey seal that had lost most of its stuffing and all of its fur. There was a scarlet ribbon round its neck which made its nudity seem obscene. The ribbon originally had come into her keeping when it had been struck in an intricate knot as an ornament on a heart-shaped box of chocolates. She had treasured the empty box, but eventually someone had thrown it away. The seal looked stupid in such a big bow, and she took it off.

The volume of Lucy's protest from the bedroom increased. Kate's frown deepened as she hurried off in the direction of the sound. She lifted the baby from the cot. Goodness, but she was heavy! She staggered back with her to the play room and dumped her down unceremoniously into the shabby rocking chair. "There!" she said. "Now you shut up!"

She gave her attention to the remnant of the pile of toys which she had not so far arranged. There were teddy bears, a giraffe, a golliwog that she had never liked, a seedy clown who had lost an arm, and "Othello"—of whose shield only the lower half had survived.

Lucy continued to scream stridently and Kate grew more and more impatient. Unless she could stop her making such a noise the couple on the floor above would come down and complain. She could not understand why Mummy and Daddy had wanted to have Lucy in the first

place. She had made the flat overcrowded, and they had
been so much happier when they had just been the four,
before Lucy had been thrust on to them.

"Lucy Locket" and "Kitty Fisher"! Such a ridiculous
jingle, which meant nothing. Kate hated the name "Kitty"
that had been foisted on to her all because of Lucy. She
detested being put into a bracket.

It was chilly without her dressing gown. She turned on
the electric "puffer" which, it had been impressed on her,
was so much safer than a fire, and the room grew alive
with its comfortable warming purr. She gave Lucy a none
too gentle shake. "Stop it!" she said. What an odious fat
lump she was, with her chubby vacant face and those
senseless blue eyes that were supposed to be like Daddy's,
only of course they weren't!

She realized dimly that one reason for her dislike of her
baby sister must be due to her parents' maddening habit
of "typing" their children. Hubert was the son and heir,
the golden boy, and there she could not fault their choice.
She herself had been labelled the "interesting" one, quaint
and amusing, to be petted and teased and shown off, anyway until she grew bigger and was no longer cute. Lucy,
it seemed, was to be the glamour girl, the song-bird . . .
the new sensation.

She jerked Lucy more upright so that her back rested
against the rubber-leather cushion. Startled, the baby,
with eyes rounding from the shock, relapsed into temporary silence. Kate left her and continued her arrangement of the toys. When they had all been set in place she
would bring into motion the actors on the stage. She
planted the unpopular golliwog directly behind "Othello"
in a row by himself so that he would have the worst view
of all. Where it had been possible the toys' heads had
been twisted, or their bodies so arranged, that they were
lined up with their faces turned expectantly towards the
performers.

The sound of young men's voices calling to one another, shouting and laughing as they prepared to disperse

to their various homes and lodgings, came up from the Square below.

"See you in the morning."

"More's the pity!"

"Bloody wage slaves—that's all we are!"

"What do you expect? Like to live like "007" on ten ruddy quid a week? See yourself as a bleedin' Casanova, eh, Dan?"

"Who wouldn't like to live like James Bond?" a fresh voice joined in.

"Old Dan may have the inclination, but he hasn't got the equipment!" There was a burst of laughter.

"How do you know what I've got?"

The heavy badinage petered out. " 'Night, then."

" 'Night, Roy. 'Night, Dan. Don't do anything I wouldn't do!"

Kate straightened up. The ribbon from the chocolate box dangled limply from her hand. She was barely in time to grab at Lucy who infuriatingly had slipped forward in the rocking chair and was in imminent danger of falling to the floor. Kate's automatic and precipitate jump to save her immediately evoked a further outcry.

The little girl clutched at her arm and, picking her up, carried her over to the table where she laid her on its scoured top, her long nightdress hanging down over the edge. Then she climbed up beside her and took her on to her knee. Kate's smooth curtain of hair flopped down over one side of her dissolute Madonna's face as, over the baby's head, she looked out at her well-drilled and intent audience.

She tossed her hair back and started to address the assembled company. "Ladies and gentlemen," she said. "You will shortly be seeing my All-Star production of *Cinderella*. There will be free ices in the interval and sweets can be had on request from the attendants." Kate was enjoying herself. Half-forgotten snatches of show-business conversation which she had heard from her parents and their visitors now came to mind. "I think you will agree that Caroline as 'Cinderella' gives a beautiful performance," she told the dolls. "Although we have not had the advantage of a provincial try-out we are not under-rehearsed and there are no rough passages." She repeated the sentence with precision, separating each syllable.

Lucy started to cry again and Kate held her more firmly. Her free hand was raising and lowering the red ribbon like a yo-yo in front of Lucy's face to quiet and amuse her, and then, almost unthinkingly as if she were playing with one of the dolls, she tied it idly round the baby's neck. Lucy stopped crying, the tears arrested on her cheeks.

Kate looked down at her with distaste. How could Daddy enjoy holding her? She was about as lovable as a sack stuffed with warm moist sand. She could hardly bring herself to touch her. Before Lucy had been born it had been Kate who had been the baby, Kate who had been tickled and played with and who had been the center of attention and now, with the advent of "Lucy Locket", everything had changed for the worse.

She shook back her hair once more and fixed her captive audience with a compelling eye. "Before the pantomime begins I would like to give you a song," she said. She spoke sternly in case there might be rebellious opposition. When none was forthcoming she began to sing in a voice that was small but sweet and true with an undertone of heartbreak. " 'Lucy Locket lost her pocket, Kitty Fisher found it; there was not a penny in it, but a ribbon round it.' "

She inclined her head in gracious recognition of imaginary applause and sang the song through again, this time not as a lullaby but with animated syncopation, gazing out gravely at the irregular semicircle of the toys, and as she sang she started to pull experimentally on the red ribbon, gradually drawing it more and more resolutely around Lucy's neck. She refused to look down at her but continued to tighten the strip of woven scarlet silk with even greater force and concentration as she became conscious of the agonized convulsive movements and feeble struggles of the small figure in her lap. She continued to chant the refrain over and over again with extemporary variations until all signs of Lucy's spasms had ceased. Only then did she allow herself to glance slowly and impersonally, without any expression except perhaps one of doubtful inquiry, at the congested face of the baby that she cradled. Almost of their own volition her fingers made the red ribbon into a neat bow. The small body in the winceyette nightgown had grown as still and as limp as any among the ranks of the inane audience.

Kate slithered down from the table and, reaching up, carried her burden over to where the regal "Othello" sat arrogantly splay-legged. She lowered the dead baby on to the throne formed by the angle of his walnut-colored thighs with his kapok-stuffed stomach and barrel chest, propping up Lucy's lolling head against the broken shield of zebra skin.

Kate was smiling, filled with a glow of peace and achievement. She lifted the hem of her nightdress and began to dance with gay formal steps around the rim of the audience of watching dolls. " 'Lucy Locket's lost her pocket . . . Kitty Fisher found it . . .' " Her voice was much better than Lucy's would ever have been, that she knew, and when he heard her sing Daddy would have to admit that it was so.

She broke off abruptly as she heard the scratch of a key in the front door. She stood stock-still waiting to see who it might be. Then she relaxed. It would be Hubert. It could be no one else. Except for her parents nobody else had a key. There came the click of footsteps on the parquet of the hall, and as the half-opened door of the play room was pushed inward she resumed her interrupted dance. Darling Hubert was another one who did not know how talented she was. She must show him. "There was not a penny in it, but a ribbon round it'."

Her brother was standing in the doorway, his pleasant

mouth stretched in a grin as she sank before him in a
deep curtsy on to the linoleum. He clapped his hands in
encouragement. "Hello, Kitty!" he greeted her. "Bravo!
But you are a naughty cat, aren't you? Why aren't you in
bed and asleep? What's going on here? Opening night, or
merely dress rehearsal?" He came towards her, his arms
held out. "Into bed at once before they get back from
their jaunt or I'll be the one who'll catch it!"

As he squatted down on his heels to pick her up he
caught sight of the white bundle among the dolls and his
smile faded. "My God, Kitty, what in Christ's name have
you done?" He spoke hoarsely, breathlessly, as if he had
been running and was exhausted. "What's happened to
Lucy?" He was crouched forward, his weight on his
hands, staring over incredulously at the Zulu doll.

Lucy might have been some child sacrifice, strangled
on a heathen altar. The grouping of the dolls was suddenly sinister. Hubert's mind refused to function. Nothing
was any more what it appeared to be. The play room in
which he had spent so great a part of his early life had
grown unreal and threatening, and beguiling Kitty, affec-
tionate little Kitty Fisher, was transformed into a dwarf
priestess of a vile and unthinkable cult, her innocent
child's face a devil's mask behind which was concealed
lunatic evil.

Kate followed his look. Was Lucy really dead? Had she
killed Lucy deliberately? It did not seem to matter either
way, and if she was dead she wouldn't bother them any
longer. She was quiet at last, and now that she had
Hubert to herself she could get on with the game.

She would have to think up another song. "Lucy
Locket" wasn't suitable; besides, Hubert had heard her
sing the end of it. What should it be? "Oh where, oh
where has my little dog gone?"; "Hey there! you with the
stars in your eyes"? That was one of Daddy's specials. He
liked to hum it to Lucy, but she could not remember all
the words and she did not want to dry up. In the pantomime itself she would have to improvise—put her own

"Cinderella" lyrics to old tunes—and if inspiration deserted her she could always "la-la-la" to fill in the gaps. Hubert would be impressed, and she wanted to impress Hubert.

Their eyes were on a level, and Kate's were alive with secret laughter. "Silly Lucy!" she said. "She kept on crying and interrupting me, so I had to put her to sleep. You've got to be strict with her, didn't you know? She can be very wilful." She came across and touched him tentatively on his broad bony shoulder under the butcher-blue shirt. "She's quiet now. We'll take her back to the night nursery. Don't you think that would be best? And then I'll do *Cinderella* all for *you*. There's plenty of time. They won't be back for hours." Her inviting look slid away from his set, horrified expression. She knew that she was in disgrace. "If you want to know," she said, "I ... I was acting that stupid song they're always crooning, 'Lucy Locket' and it ... it just happened. It was a good idea of mine, wasn't it?"

Hubert made no reply and she considered it wiser to change the subject. She took her hand away from his shoulder and asked in a conversational adult manner. "And how was Hermione, Hubert? Do tell me ... is she nice?" Kate's eyes searched his face. "Do you like her very much?" Her lips curved in their practised smile. "Do you like her more than you like me?"

The Treader
of the Dust

Clark Ashton Smith

Mr. Clark Ashton Smith's reputation is growing steadily and may some day approach what he has all along deserved. Here is his vision of a terrifying entity whose awfulness lies not so much in its supreme deadliness, but in its dreadful indifference.

... The olden wizards knew him, and named him Quachil Uttaus. Seldom is he revealed; for he dwelleth beyond the outermost circle, in the dark limbo of unsphered time and space. Dreadful is the word that calleth him, though the word be unspoken save in thought: For Quachil Uttaus is the ultimate corruption; and the instant of his coming is like the passage of many ages; and neither flesh nor stone may abide his treading, but all things crumble beneath it atom from atom. And for this, some have called him The Treader of the Dust.

—*The Testaments of Carnamagos.*

 T WAS AFTER interminable debate and argument with himself, after many attempts to exorcise the dim, bodiless legion of his fears, that John Sebastian returned to the house he had left so hurriedly. He had been absent only for three days: but even this was an interruption without precedent in the life of reclusion and study to which he had given himself completely following his inheritance of the old mansion together with a

generous income. At no time would he have defined fully
the reason of his flight: nevertheless, flight had seemed
imperative. There was some horrible urgency that had
driven him forth; but now, since he had determined to go
back, the urgency was resolved into a matter of nerves
overwrought by too close and prolonged application to his
books. He had fancied certain things: but the fancies were
patently absurd and baseless.

Even if the phenomena that had perturbed him were
not all imaginary, there must be some natural solution
that had not occurred to his overheated mind at the time.
The sudden yellowing of a newly purchased notebook, the
crumbling of the sheets at their edges, were no doubt due
to a latent imperfection of the paper; and the queer fading
of his entries, which, almost overnight, had become faint
as age-old writing, was clearly the result of cheap, faulty
chemicals in the ink. The aspect of sheer, brittle, worm-
hollowed antiquity which had manifested itself in certain
articles of furniture, certain portions of the mansion, was
no more than the sudden revealing of a covert disinte-
gration that had gone on unnoticed by him in his sedulous
application to dark but absorbing researches. And it was
this same application, with its unbroken years of toil and
confinement, which had brought about his premature ag-
ing; so that, looking into the mirror on the morn of his
flight, he had been startled and shocked as if by the appa-
rition of a withered mummy. As to the man-servant, Timmers—well, Timmers had been old ever since he could
remember. It was only the exaggeration of sick nerves
that had lately found in Timmers a decrepitude so extreme that it might fall, without the intermediacy of death,
at any moment, into the corruption of the grave.

Indeed, he could explain all that had troubled him
without reference to the wild, remote lore, the forgotten
demonologies and systems into which he had delved.
Those passages in *The Testaments of Carnamagos,* over
which he had pondered with weird dismay, were relevant

only to the horrors evoked by mad sorcerers in bygone
eons. . . .

Sebastian, firm in such convictions, came back at sunset
to his house. He did not tremble or falter as he crossed
the pine-darkened grounds and ran quickly up the front
steps. He fancied, but could not be sure, that there were
fresh signs of dilapidation in the steps; and the house itself, as he approached it, had seemed to lean a little
aslant, as if from some ruinous settling of the foundations: but this, he told himself, was an illusion wrought by
the gathering twilight.

No lamps had been lit, but Sebastian was not unduly
surprised by this, for he knew that Timmers, left to his
own devices, was prone to dodder about in the gloom like
a senescent owl, long after the proper time of lamp-light-
ing. Sebastian, on the other hand, had always been averse
to darkness or even deep shadow; and of late the aversion
had increased upon him. Invariably he turned on all the
bulbs in the house as soon as the daylight began to fail.
Now, muttering his irritation at Timmers' remissness, he
pushed open the door and reached hurriedly for the hall
switch.

Because, perhaps, of a nervous agitation which he
would not own to himself, he fumbled for several moments without finding the knob. The hall was strangely
dark, and a glimmering from the ashen sunset, sifted between tall pines into the doorway behind him, was seemingly powerless to penetrate beyond its threshold. He
could see nothing; it was as if the night of dead ages had
laired in that hallway; and his nostrils, while he stood
groping, were assailed by a dry pungency as of ancient
dust, an odor as of corpses and coffins long indistinguishable in powdery decay.

At last he found the switch; but the illumination that
responded was somehow dim and insufficient, and he
seemed to detect a shadowy flickering, as if the circuit
were at fault. However, it reassured him to see that the
house, to all appearance, was very much as he had left it.

Perhaps, unconsciously, he had feared to find the oaken panels crumbling away in riddled rottenness, the carpet falling into moth-eaten tatters; had apprehended the breaking through of rotted boards beneath his tread.

Where, he wondered now, was Timmers? The aged factotum, in spite of his growing senility, had always been quick to appear; and even if he had not heard his master enter, the switching on of the lights would have signalized Sebastian's return to him. But, though Sebastian listened with painful intentness, there was no creaking of the familiar tottery footsteps. Silence hung everywhere like a funereal, unstirred arras.

No doubt, Sebastian thought, there was some commonplace explanation. Timmers had gone to the near-by village, perhaps to restock the larder, or in hope of receiving a letter from his master; and Sebastian had missed him on the way home from the station. Or perhaps the old man had fallen ill and was now lying helpless in his room. Filled with this latter thought, he went straight to Timmers' bedchamber, which was on the ground floor, at the back of the mansion. It was empty, and the bed was neatly made and had obviously not been occupied since the night before. With a suspiration of relief that seemed to lift a horrid incubus from his bosom, he decided that his first conjecture had been correct.

Now, pending the return of Timmers, he nerved himself to another act of inspection, and went forthwith into his study. He would not admit to himself precisely what it was that he had feared to see; but at first glance, the room was unchanged, and all things were as they had been at the time of his flurried departure. The confused and high-piled litter of manuscripts, volumes, notebooks on his writing-table had seemingly lain untouched by anything but his own hand; and his bookshelves, with their bizarre and terrific array of authorities on diabolism, necromancy, goety, on all the ridiculed or outlawed sciences, were undisturbed and intact. On the old lecturn or reading-stand which he used for his heavier tomes, *The Testa-*

ments of Carnamagos, in its covers of shagreen with hasps of human bone, lay open at the very page which had frightened him so unreasonably with its eldritch intimations.

Then, as he stepped forward between the reading-stand and the table, he perceived for the first time the inexplicable *dustiness* of everything. Dust lay everywhere: a fine gray dust like a powder of dead atoms. It had covered his manuscripts with a deep film, it had settled thickly upon the chairs, the lamp-shades, the volumes; and the rich poppy-like reds and yellows of the oriental rugs were bedimmed by its accumulation. It was as if many desolate years had passed through the chamber since his own departure, and had shaken from their shroud-like garments the dust of all ruined things. The mystery of it chilled Sebastian: for he knew that the room had been clean-swept only three days previous; and Timmers would have dusted the place each morning with meticulous care during his absence.

Now the dust rose up in a light, swirling cloud about him, it filled his nostrils with the same dry odor, as of fantastically ancient dissolution, that had met him in the hall. At the same moment he grew aware of a cold, gusty draft that had somehow entered the room. He thought that one of the windows must have been left open, but a glance assured him that they were shut, with tightly drawn blinds; and the door was closed behind him. The draft was light as the sighing of a phantom, but wherever it passed, the fine, weightless powder soared aloft, filling the air and settling again with utmost slowness. Sebastian felt a weird alarm, as if a wind had blown upon him from chartless dimensions, or through some hidden rift of ruin; and simultaneously he was seized by a paroxysm of prolonged and violent coughing.

He could not locate the source of the draft. But, as he moved restlessly about, his eye was caught by a low long mound of the gray dust, which had heretofore been hidden from view by the table. It lay beside the chair in which he usually sat while writing. Near the heap was the feather-duster used by Timmers in his daily round of house-cleaning.

It seemed to Sebastian that the rigor of a great, lethal coldness had invaded all his being. He could not stir for several minutes, but stood peering down at the inexplicable mound. In the center of that mound he saw a vague depression, which might have been the mark of a very small footprint half erased by the gusts of air that had evidently taken much of the dust and scattered it about the chamber.

At last the power of motion returned to Sebastian. Without conscious recognition of the impulse that prompted him, he bent forward to pick up the feather-duster. But, even as his fingers touched it, the handle and the feathers crumbled into fine powder which, settling in a low pile, preserved vaguely the outlines of the original object.

A weakness came upon Sebastian, as if the burden of utter age and mortality had gathered crushingly on his shoulders between one instant and the next. There was a whirling of vertiginous shadows before his eyes in the lamplight, and he felt that he should swoon unless he sat down immediately. He put out his hand to reach the chair beside him—and the chair, at his touch, fell instantly into light, downward-sifting clouds of dust.

Afterward—how long afterward he could not tell—he found himself sitting in the high chair before the lectern on which *The Testaments of Carnamagos* lay open. Dimly he was surprised that the seat had not crumbled beneath him. Upon him, as once before, there was the urgency of swift, sudden flight from that accursed house: but it seemed that he had grown too old, too weary and feeble; and that nothing mattered greatly—not even the grisly doom which he apprehended.

Now, as he sat there in a state half terror, half stupor, his eyes were drawn to the wizard volume before him: the writings of that evil sage and seer, Carnamagos, which

had been recovered a thousand years agone from some
Graeco-Bactrian tomb, and transcribed by an apostate
monk in the original Greek, in the blood of an incubus-be-
gotten monster. In that volume were the chronicles of
great sorcerers of old, and the histories of demons earthly
and ultra-cosmic, and the veritable spells by which the
demons could be called up and controlled and dismissed.
Sebastian, a profound student of such lore, had long believed that the book was a mere medieval legend; and he
had been startled as well as gratified when he found this
copy on the shelves of a dealer in old manuscripts and in-
cunabula. It was said that only two copies had ever existed, and that the other had been destroyed by the Spanish
Inquisition early in the Thirteenth Century.

The light flickered as if ominous wings had flown
across it; and Sebastian's eyes blurred with a gathering
rheum as he read again that sinister, fatal passage which
had served to provoke shadowy fears:

Though Quachil Uttaus cometh but rarely, it hath been well
attested that his advent is not always in response to the spoken
rune and the drawn pentacle. . . . Few wizards, indeed, would
call upon a spirit so baleful. . . . But let it be understood that
he who readeth to himself, in the silence of his chamber, the
formula given hereunder, must incur a grave risk if in his
heart there abide openly or hidden the least desire of death
and annihilation. For it may be that Quachil Uttaus will come
to him, bringing that doom which toucheth the body to eternal
dust, and maketh the soul as a vapor for evermore dissolved.
And the advent of Quachil Uttaus is foreknowable by certain
tokens: for in the person of the evocator, and even perchance
in those about him, will appear the signs of sudden age; and
his house, and those belongings which he hath touched, will
assume the marks of untimely decay and antiquity. . . .

Sebastian did not know that he was mumbling the sen-
tences half aloud as he read them; that he was also mumbling the terrible incantation that followed. . . . His
thoughts crawled as if through a chill and freezing

medium. With a dull, ghastly certainty, he knew Timmers had not gone to the village. He should have warned Timmers before leaving; he should have closed and locked *The Testaments of Carnamagos* ... for Timmers, in his way, was something of a scholar and was not without curiosity concerning the occult studies of his master. Timmers was well able to read the Greek of Carnamagos ... even that dire and soul-blasting formula to which Quachil Uttaus, demon of ultimate corruption, would respond from the outer void. ... Too well Sebastian divined the origin of the gray dust, the reason of those mysterious crumblings. ...

Again he felt the impulse of flight: but his body was a dry dead incubus that refused to obey his volition. Anyway, he reflected, it was too late now, for the signs of doom had gathered about him and upon him. ... Yet, surely there had never been in his heart the least longing for death and destruction. He had wished only to pursue his delvings into the blacker mysteries that environed the mortal estate. And he had always been cautious, had never cared to meddle with magic circles and evocations of perilous presences. He had known that there were spirits of evil, spirits of wrath, perdition, annihilation: but never, of his own will, should he have summoned any of them from their night-bound abysms. ...

His lethargy and weakness seemed to increase: it was as if whole lustrums, whole decades of senescence had fallen upon him in the drawing of a breath. The thread of his thoughts was broken at intervals, and he recovered it with difficulty. His memories, even his fears, seemed to totter on the edge of some final forgetfulness. With dulled ears he heard a sound as of timbers breaking and falling somewhere in the house; with dimmed eyes like those of an ancient he saw the lights waver and go out beneath the swooping of a bat-black darkness.

It was as if the night of some crumbling catacomb had closed upon him. He felt at whiles the chill faint breathing of the draft that had troubled him before with its mystery;

and again the dust rose up in his nostrils. Then he realized that the room was not wholly dark, for he could discern the dim outlines of the lectern before him. Surely no ray was admitted by the drawn window-blinds: yet somehow there was light. His eyes, lifting with enormous effort, saw for the first time that a rough, irregular gap had appeared in the room's outer wall, high up in the north corner. Through it, a single star shone into the chamber, cold and remote as the eye of a demon glaring across intercosmic gulfs.

Out of that star—or from the spaces beyond it—a beam of livid radiance, wan and deathly, was hurled like a spear upon Sebastian. Broad as a plank, unwavering, immovable, it seemed to transfix his very body and to form a bridge between himself and the worlds of unimagined darkness.

He was as one petrified by the gaze of the Gorgon. Then, through the aperture of ruin, there came something that glided stiffly and rapidly into the room toward him, along the beam. The wall seemed to crumble, the rift widened as it entered.

It was a figure no larger than a young child, but sere and shriveled as some millennial mummy. Its hairless head, its unfeatured face, borne on a neck of skeleton thinness, were lined with a thousand reticulated wrinkles. The body was like that of some monstrous, withered abortion that had never drawn breath. The pipy arms, ending in bony claws, were outthrust as if ankylosed in the posture of an eternal dreadful groping. The legs, with feet like those of a pigmy Death, were drawn tightly together as though confined by the swathings of the tomb; nor was there any movement of striding or pacing. Upright and rigid, the horror floated swiftly down the wan, deathly gray beam toward Sebastian.

Now it was close upon him, its head level with his brow and its feet opposite his bosom. For a fleeting moment he knew that the horror had touched him with its outflung hands, with its starkly floating feet. It seemed to merge within him, to become one with his being. He felt that his veins were choked with dust, that his brain was crumbling cell by cell. Then he was no longer John Sebastian, but a universe of dead stars and worlds that fell eddying into darkness before the tremendous blowing of some ultrastellar wind. . . .

The thing that immemorial wizards had named Quachil Uttaus was gone; and night and starlight had returned to that ruinous chamber. But nowhere was there any shadow of John Sebastian: only a low mound of dust on the floor beside the lecturn, bearing a vague depression like the imprint of a small foot . . . or of two feet that were pressed closely together.

The Horror of the Heights

Sir Arthur Conan Doyle

This is a grand demonstration that if you do this kind of story well, it has fantastic survivability. The question here asked has long been answered, the dreadful thesis advanced is hopelessly outdated, and yet I'll bet you think of it at some point during your next supersonic flight and look up.

(WHICH INCLUDES THE MS. KNOWN AS THE JOYCE-ARMSTRONG FRAGMENT)

HE IDEA that the extraordinary narrative which has been called the Joyce-Armstrong Fragment is an elaborate practical joke evolved by some unknown person, cursed by a perverted and sinister sense of humor, has now been abandoned by all who have examined the matter. The most *macabre* and imaginative of plotters would hesitate before linking his morbid fancies with the unquestioned and tragic facts which reinforce the statement. Though the assertions contained in it are amazing and even monstrous, it is none the less forcing itself upon the general intelligence that they are true, and that we must readjust our ideas to the new situation. This world of ours appears to be separated by a slight and precarious margin of safety from a most singular and unexpected danger. I will endeavor in this narrative, which reproduces the original document in its necessarily somewhat fragmentary form, to lay before the reader the whole of the facts up to date, prefacing my statement by saying that, if there be any who doubt the narrative of Joyce-Armstrong, there can be no question at all as to the facts

FAVORITE TALES OF HORROR

concerning Lieutenant Myrtle, R.N., and Mr. Hay Connor, who undoubtedly met their end in the manner described.

The Joyce-Armstrong Fragment was found in the field which is called Lower Haycock, lying one mile to the westward of the village of Withyham, upon the Kent and Sussex border. It was on the fifteenth of September last that an agricultural laborer, James Flynn, in the employment of Mathew Dodd, farmer, of the Chauntry Farm, Withyham, perceived a briar pipe lying near the footpath which skirts the hedge in Lower Haycock. A few paces farther on he picked up a pair of broken binocular glasses. Finally, among some nettles in the ditch, he caught sight of a flat, canvas-backed book, which proved to be a note-book with detachable leaves, some of which had come loose and were fluttering along the base of the hedge. These he collected, but some, including the first, were never recovered, and leave a deplorable hiatus in this all-important statement. The note-book was taken by the laborer to his master, who in turn showed it to Dr. J. H. Atherton, of Hartfield. This gentleman at once recognized the need for an expert examination, and the manuscript was forwarded to the Aero Club in London, where it now lies.

The first two pages of the manuscript are missing. There is also one torn away at the end of the narrative, though none of these affect the general coherence of the story. It is conjectured that the missing opening is concerned with the record of Mr. Joyce-Armstrong's qualifications as an aeronaut, which can be gathered from other sources and are admitted to be unsurpassed among the air-pilots of England. For many years he has been looked upon as among the most daring and the most intellectual of flying men, a combination which has enabled him to both invent and test several new devices, including the common gyroscopic attachment which is known by his name. The main body of the manuscript is written neatly in ink, but the last few lines are in pencil and are so ragged as to be hardly legible—exactly, in fact, as they might be expected to appear if they were scribbled off hurriedly from the seat of a moving airplane. There are, it may be added, several stains, both on the last page and on the outside cover which have been pronounced by the Home Office experts to be blood—probably human and certainly mammalian. The fact that something closely resembling the organism of malaria was discovered in this blood, and that Joyce-Armstrong is known to have suffered from intermittent fever, is a remarkable example of the new weapons which modern science has placed in the hands of our detectives.

And now a word as to the personality of the author of this epoch-making statement. Joyce-Armstrong, according to the few friends who really knew something of the man, was a poet and a dreamer, as well as a mechanic and an inventor. He was a man of considerable wealth, much of which he had spent in the pursuit of his aero-nautical hobby. He had four private airplanes in his hangars near Devizes, and is said to have made no fewer than one hundred and seventy ascents in the course of last year. He was a retiring man with dark moods, in which he would avoid the society of his fellows. Captain Dangerfield, who knew him better than anyone, says that there were times when his eccentricity threatened to develop into something more serious. His habit of carrying a shot-gun with him in his airplane was one manifestation of it.

Another was the morbid effect which the fall of Lieutenant Myrtle had upon his mind. Myrtle, who was attempting the height record, fell from an altitude of something over thirty thousand feet. Horrible to narrate, his head was entirely obliterated, though his body and limbs preserved their configuration. At every gathering of airmen, Joyce-Armstrong, according to Dangerfield, would ask, with an enigmatic smile: "And where, pray, is Myrtle's head?"

On another occasion after dinner, at the mess of the Flying School on Salisbury Plain, he started a debate as to what will be the most permanent danger which airmen will have to encounter. Having listened to successive opinions as to air-pockets, faulty construction, and over-banking, he ended by shrugging his shoulders and refusing to put forward his own views, though he gave the impression that they differed from any advanced by his companions.

It is worth remarking that after his own complete disappearance it was found that his private affairs were arranged with a precision which may show that he had a strong premonition of disaster. With these essential explanations I will now give the narrative exactly as it stands, beginning at page three of the blood-soaked notebook:—

"Nevertheless, when I dined at Rheims with Coselli and Gustav Raymond I found that neither of them was aware of any particular danger in the higher layers of the atmosphere. I did not actually say what was in my thoughts, but I got so near to it that if they had any corresponding idea they could not have failed to express it. But then they are two empty, vainglorious fellows with no thought beyond seeing their silly names in the newspaper. It is interesting to note that neither of them had ever been much beyond the twenty-thousand-foot level. Of course, men have been higher than this both in balloons and in the ascent of mountains. It must be well above that point that the airplane enters the danger zone—always presuming that my premonitions are correct.

"Aeroplaning has been with us now for more than twenty years, and one might well ask: Why should this peril be only revealing itself in our day? The answer is obvious. In the old days of weak engines, when a hundred horse-power Gnome or Green was considered ample for every need, the flights were very restricted. Now that three hundred horse-power is the rule rather than the exception, visits to the upper layers have become easier and more common. Some of us can remember how, in our

youth, Garros made a world-wide reputation by attaining
nineteen thousand feet, and it was considered a remarkable achievement to fly over the Alps. Our standard now
has been immeasurably raised, and there are twenty high
flights for one in former years. Many of them have been
undertaken with impunity. The thirty-thousand-foot level
has been reached time after time with no discomfort beyond cold and asthma. What does this prove? A visitor
might descend upon this planet a thousand times and
never see a tiger. Yet tigers exist, and if he chanced to
come down into a jungle he might be devoured. There are
jungles of the upper air, and there are worse things than
tigers which inhabit them. I believe in time they will map
these jungles accurately out. Even at the present moment
I could name two of them. One of them lies over the
Pau-Biarritz district of France. Another is just over my
head as I write here in my house in Wiltshire. I rather
think there is a third in the Homburg-Wiesbaden district.

"It was the disappearance of the airmen that first set
me thinking. Of course, everyone said that they had fallen
into the sea, but that did not satisfy me at all. First, there
was Verrier in France; his machine was found near Bay-
onne, but they never got his body. There was the case of
Baxter also, who vanished, though his engine and some
of the iron fixings were found in a wood in Leicestershire.
In that case, Dr. Middleton, of Amesbury, who was
watching the flight with a telescope, declares that just before the clouds obscured the view he saw the machine,
which was at an enormous height, suddenly rise perpendi-
cularly upwards in a succession of jerks in a manner that
he would have thought to be impossible. That was the last
seen of Baxter. There was a correspondence in the papers, but it never led to anything. There were several
other similar cases, and then there was the death of Hay
Connor. What a cackle there was about an unsolved mystery of the air, and what columns in the halfpenny papers,
and yet how little was ever done to get to the bottom of
the business! He came down in a tremendous vol-plané

from an unknown height. He never got off his machine and died in his pilot's seat. Died of what? 'Heart disease,' said the doctors. Rubbish! Hay Connor's heart was as sound as mine is. What did Venables say? Venables was the only man who was at his side when he died. He said that he was shivering and looked like a man who had been badly scared. 'Died of fright,' said Venables, but could not imagine what he was frightened about. Only said one word to Venables, which sounded like 'Monstrous.' They could make nothing of that at the inquest. But I could make something of it. Monsters! That was the last word of poor Harry Hay Connor. And he *did* die of fright, just as Venables thought.

"And then there was Myrtle's head. Do you really believe—does anybody really believe—that a man's head could be driven clean into his body by the force of a fall? Well, perhaps it may be possible, but I, for one, have never believed that it was so with Myrtle. And the grease upon his clothes—'all slimy with grease,' said somebody at the inquest. Queer that nobody got thinking after that! I did—but, then, I had been thinking for a good long time. I've made three ascents—how Dangerfield used to chaff me about my shot-gun—but I've never been high enough. Now, with this new, light Paul Veroner machine and its one hundred and seventy-five Robur, I should easily touch the thirty thousand tomorrow. I'll have a shot at the record. Maybe I shall have a shot at something else as well. Of course, it's dangerous. If a fellow wants to avoid danger he had best keep out of flying altogether and subside finally into flannel slippers and a dressing-gown. But I'll visit the air-jungle tomorrow—and if there's anything there I shall know it. If I return, I'll find myself a bit of a celebrity. If I don't, this note-book may explain what I am trying to do, and how I lost my life in doing it. But no drivel about accidents or mysteries, if *you* please.

"I chose my Paul Veroner monoplane for the job. There's nothing like a monoplane when real work is to be done. Beaumont found that out in very early days. For

one thing it doesn't mind damp, and the weather looks as
if we should be in the clouds all the time. It's a bonny
little model and answers my hand like a tender-mouthed
horse. The engine is a ten-cylinder rotary Robur working
up to one hundred and seventy-five. It has all the modern
improvements—enclosed fuselage, high-curved landing
skids, brakes, gyroscopic steadiers, and three speeds,
worked by an alteration of the angle of the planes upon
the Venetian-blind principle. I took a shot-gun with me
and a dozen cartridges filled with buck-shot. You should
have seen the face of Perkins, my old mechanic, when I
directed him to put them in. I was dressed like an Arctic
explorer, with two jerseys under my overalls, thick socks
inside my padded boots, a storm-cap with flaps, and my
talc goggles. It was stifling outside the hangars, but I was
going for the summit of the Himalayas, and had to dress
for the part. Perkins knew there was something on and
implored me to take him with me. Perhaps I should if I
were using the biplane, but a monoplane is a one-man
show—if you want to get the last foot of lift out of it. Of
course, I took an oxygen bag; the man who goes for the
altitude record without one will either be frozen or smothered—or both.

"I had a good look at the planes, the rudder-bar, and
the elevating lever before I got in. Everything was in order so far as I could see. Then I switched on my engine
and found that she was running sweetly. When they let
her go she rose almost at once upon the lowest speed. I
circled my home field once or twice just to warm her up,
and then, with a wave to Perkins and the others, I flat-
tened out my planes and put her on her highest. She
skimmed like a swallow down wind for eight or ten miles
until I turned her nose up a little and she began to climb
in a great spiral for the cloud-bank above me. It's all-important to rise slowly and adapt yourself to the pressure
as you go.

"It was a close, warm day for an English September,
and there was the hush and heaviness of impending rain.

Now and then there came sudden puffs of wind from the south-west—one of them so gusty and unexpected that it caught me napping and turned me half-round for an instant. I remember the time when gusts and whirls and air-pockets used to be things of danger—before we learned to put an overmastering power into our engines. Just as I reached the cloud-banks, with the altimeter marking three thousand, down came the rain. My word, how it poured! It drummed upon my wings and lashed against my face, blurring my glasses so that I could hardly see. I got down on to a low speed, for it was painful to travel against it. As I got higher it became hail, and I had to turn tail to it. One of my cylinders was out of action—a dirty plug, I should imagine, but still I was rising steadily with plenty of power. After a bit the trouble passed, whatever it was, and I heard the full, deep-throated purr—the ten singing as one. That's where the beauty of our modern silencers comes in. We can at last control our engines by ear. How they squeal and squeak and sob when they are in trouble! All those cries for help were wasted in the old days, when every sound was swallowed up by the monstrous racket of the machine. If only the early aviators could come back to see the beauty and perfection of the mechanism which have been bought at the cost of their lives!

"About nine-thirty I was nearing the clouds. Down below me, all blurred and shadowed with rain, lay the vast expanse of Salisbury Plain. Half a dozen flying machines were doing hackwork at the thousand-foot level, looking like little black swallows against the green background. I dare say they were wondering what I was doing up in cloud-land. Suddenly a grey curtain drew across beneath me and the wet folds of vapors were swirling round my face. It was clammily cold and miserable. But I was above the hail-storm, and that was something gained. The cloud was as dark and thick as a London fog. In my anxiety to get clear, I cocked her nose up until the automatic alarm-bell rang, and I actually began to slide backwards.

My sopped and dripping wings had made me heavier than I thought, but presently I was in lighter cloud, and soon had cleared the first layer. There was a second—opal-coloured and fleecy—at a great height above my head, a white, unbroken ceiling above, and a dark, unbroken floor below, with the monoplane laboring upwards upon a vast spiral between them. It is deadly lonely in these cloud-spaces. Once a great flight of some small water-birds went past me, flying very fast to the westwards. The quick whir of their wings and their musical cry were cheery to my ear. I fancy that they were teal, but I am a wretched zoologist. Now that we humans have become birds we must really learn to know our brethren by sight.

"The wind down beneath me whirled and swayed the broad cloud-plain. Once a great eddy formed in it, a whirlpool of vapor, and through it, as down a funnel, I caught sight of the distant world. A large white biplane was passing at a vast depth beneath me. I fancy it was the morning mail service betwixt Bristol and London. Then the drift swirled inwards again and the great solitude was unbroken.

"Just after ten I touched the lower edge of the upper cloud-stratum. It consisted of fine diaphanous vapor drifting swiftly from the westward. The wind had been steadily rising all this time and it was now blowing a sharp breeze—twenty-eight an hour by my guage. Already it was very cold, though my altimeter only marked nine thousand. The engines were working beautifully, and we went droning steadily upwards. The cloud-bank was thicker than I had expected, but at last it thinned out into a golden mist before me, and then in an instant I had shot out from it, and there was an unclouded sky and a brilliant sun above my head—all blue and gold above, all shining silver below, one vast, glimmering plain as far as my eyes could reach. It was a quarter past ten o'clock, and the barograph needle pointed to twelve thousand eight hundred. Up I went and up, my ears concentrated upon the deep purring of my motor, my eyes busy always with the watch, the revolution indicator, the petrol lever, and the oil pump. No wonder aviators are said to be a fearless race. With so many things to think of there is no time to trouble about oneself. About this time I noted how unreliable is the compass when above a certain height from earth. At fifteen thousand feet mine was pointing east and a point south. The sun and the wind gave me my true bearings.

I had hoped to reach an eternal stillness in these high altitudes, but with every thousand feet of ascent the gale grew stronger. My machine groaned and trembled in every joint and rivet as she faced it, and swept away like a sheet of paper when I banked her on the turn, skimmering down wind at a greater pace, perhaps, than ever mortal man has moved. Yet I had always to turn again and tack up in the wind's eye, for it was not merely a height record that I was after. But all my calculations it was above little Wiltshire that my air-jungle lay, and all my labor might be lost if I struck the outer layers at some farther point.

"When I reached the nineteen-thousand-foot level, which was about midday, the wind was so severe that I looked with some anxiety to the stays of my wings, expecting momentarily to see them snap or slacken. I even cast loose the parachute behind me, and fastened its hook into the ring of my leathern belt, so as to be ready for the worst. Now was the time when a bit of scamped work by the mechanic is paid for by the life of the aeronaut. But she held together bravely. Every cord and strut was humming and vibrating like so many harp-strings, but it was glorious to see how, for all the beating and the buffeting, she was still the conqueror of Nature and the mistress of the sky. There is surely something divine in man himself that he should rise so superior to the limitations which Creation seemed to impose—rise, too, by such unselfish, heroic devotion as this air-conquest has shown. Talk of human degeneration! When has such a story as this been written in the annals of our race?

"These were the thoughts in my head as I climbed that monstrous, inclined plane with the wind sometimes beating in my face and sometimes whistling behind my ears, while the cloud-land beneath me fell away to such a distance that the folds and hummocks of silver had all smoothed out into one flat, shining plain. But suddenly I had a horrible and unprecedented experience. I have known before what it is to be in what our neighbors have called a *tourbillon,* but never on such a scale as this. That huge, sweeping river of wind of which I have spoken had, as it appears, whirlpools within it which were as monstrous as itself. Without a moment's warning I was dragged suddenly into the heart of one. I spun round for a minute or two with such velocity that I almost lost my senses, and then fell suddenly, left wing foremost, down the vacuum tunnel in the center. I dropped like a stone, and lost nearly a thousand feet. It was only my belt that kept me in my seat, and the shock and breathlessness left me hanging half-insensible over the side of the fuselage. But I am always capable of a supreme effort—it is my one great merit as an aviator. I was conscious that the descent was slower. The whirlpool was a cone rather than a funnel, and I had come to the apex. With a terrific wrench, throwing my weight all to one side, I levelled my planes and brought her head away from the wind. In an instant I had shot out of the eddies and was skimming down the sky. Then, shaken but victorious, I turned her nose up and began once more my steady grind on the upward spiral. I took a large sweep to avoid the danger-spot of the whirlpool, and soon I was safely above it. Just after one o'clock I was twenty-one thousand feet above the sea-level. To my great joy I had topped the gale, and with every hundred feet of ascent the air grew stiller. On the other hand, it was very cold, and I was conscious of that peculiar nausea which goes with rarefaction of the air. For the first time I unscrewed the mouth of my oxygen bag and took an occasional whiff of the glorious gas. I could feel it running like a cordial through my veins, and

I was exhilarated almost to the point of drunkenness. I shouted and sang as I soared upwards into the cold, still outer world.

"It is very clear to me that the insensibility which came upon Glaisher, and in a lesser degree upon Coxwell, when, in 1862, they ascended in a balloon to the height of thirty thousand feet, was due to the extreme speed with which a perpendicular ascent is made. Doing it at an easy gradient and accustoming oneself to the lessened barometric pressure by slow degrees, there are no such dreadful symptoms. At the same great height I found that even without my oxygen inhaler I could breathe without undue distress. It was bitterly cold, however, and my thermometer was at zero, Fahrenheit. At one-thirty I was nearly seven miles above the surface of the earth, and still ascending steadily. I found, however, that the rarefied air was giving markedly less support to my planes, and that my angle of ascent had to be considerably lowered in consequence. It was already clear that even with my light weight and strong engine-power there was a point in front of me where I should be held. To make matters worse, one of my sparking-plugs was in trouble again and there was intermittent misfiring in the engine. My heart was heavy with the fear of failure.

"It was about that time that I had a most extraordinary experience. Something whizzed past me in a trail of smoke and exploded with a loud, hissing sound, sending forth a cloud of steam. For the instant I could not imagine what had happened. Then I remembered that the earth is for ever being bombarded by meteor stones, and would be hardly inhabitable were they not in nearly every case turned to vapor in the outer layers of the atmosphere. Here is a new danger for the high-altitude man, for two others passed me when I was nearing the forty-thousand-foot mark. I cannot doubt that at the edge of the earth's envelope the risk would be a very real one.

"My barograph needle marked forty-one thousand three hundred when I became aware that I could go no farther. Physically, the strain was not as yet greater than I could bear, but my machine had reached its limit. The attenuated air gave no firm support to the wings, and the least tilt developed into side-slip, while she seemed sluggish on her controls. Possibly, had the engine been at its best, another thousand feet might have been within our capacity, but it was still misfiring, and two out of the ten cylinders appeared to be out of action. If I had not already reached the zone for which I was searching then I should never see it upon this journey. But was it not possible that I had attained it? Soaring in circles like a monstrous hawk upon the forty-thousand-foot level I let the monoplane guide herself, and with my Mannheim glass I made a careful observation of my surroundings. The heavens were perfectly clear; there was no indication of those dangers which I had imagined.

"I have said that I was soaring in circles. It struck me suddenly that I would do well to take a wider sweep and open up a new air-tract. If the hunter entered an earth-jungle he would drive through it if he wished to find his game. My reasoning had led me to believe that the air-jungle which I had imagined lay somewhere over Wiltshire. This should be to the south and west of me. I took my bearings from the sun, for the compass was hopeless and no trace of earth was to be seen—nothing but the distant, silver cloud-plain. However, I got my direction as best I might and kept her head straight to the mark. I reckoned that my petrol supply would not last for more than another hour or so, but I could afford to use it to the last drop, since a single magnificent vol-plané could at any time take me to the earth.

"Suddenly I was aware of something new. The air in front of me had lost its crystal clearness. It was full of long, ragged wisps of something which I can only compare to very fine cigarette-smoke. It hung about in wreaths and coils, turning and twisting slowly in the sunlight. As the monoplane shot through it, I was aware of a faint taste of oil upon my lips, and there was a greasy scum upon the woodwork of the machine. Some infinitely fine organic matter appeared to be suspended in the atmosphere. There was no life there. It was inchoate and diffuse, extending for many square acres and then fringing off into the void. No, it was not life. But might it not be the remains of life? Above all, might it not be the food of life, of monstrous life, even as the humble grease of the ocean is the food for the mighty whale? The thought was in my mind when my eyes looked upwards and I saw the most wonderful vision that ever man has seen. Can I hope to convey it to you even as I saw it myself last Thursday?

"Conceive a jelly-fish such as sails in our summer seas, bell-shaped and of enormous size—far larger, I should judge, than the dome of St. Paul's. It was of a light pink color veined with a delicate green, but the whole huge fabric so tenuous that it was but a fairy outline against the dark blue sky. It pulsated with a delicate and regular rhythm. From it there depended two long, drooping, green tentacles, which swayed slowly backwards and forwards. This gorgeous vision passed gently with noiseless dignity over my head, as light and fragile as a soap-bubble, and drifted upon its stately way.

"I had half-turned my monoplane, that I might look after this beautiful creature, when, in a moment, I found myself amidst a perfect fleet of them, of all sizes, but none so large as the first. Some were quite small, but the majority about as big as an average balloon, and with much the same curvature at the top. There was in them a delicacy of texture and coloring which reminded me of the finest Venetian glass. Pale shades of pink and green were the prevailing tints, but all had a lovely iridescence where the sun shimmered through their dainty forms. Some hundreds of them drifted past me, a wonderful fairy squadron of strange, unknown argosies of the sky—creatures whose forms and substance were so attuned to these pure heights that one could not conceive anything so delicate within actual sight or sound of earth.

"But soon my attention was drawn to a new phenomenon—the serpents of the outer air. These were long, thin, fantastic coils of vapour-like material, which turned and twisted with great speed, flying round and round at such a pace that the eyes could hardly follow them. Some of these ghost-like creatures were twenty or thirty feet long, but it was difficult to tell their girth, for their outline was so hazy that it seemed to fade away into the air around them. These air-snakes were of a very light grey or smoke color, with some darker lines within, which gave the impression of a definite organism. One of them whisked past my very face, and I was conscious of a cold, clammy contact, but their composition was so unsubstantial that I could not connect them with any thought of physical danger, any more than the beautiful bell-like creatures which had preceded them. There was no more solidity in their frames than in the floating spume from a broken wave.

"But a more terrible experience was in store for me. Floating downwards from a great height there came a purplish patch of vapor, small as I saw it first, but rapidly enlarging as it approached me, until it appeared to be hundreds of square feet in size. Though fashioned of some transparent, jelly-like substance, it was none the less of much more definite outline and solid consistence than anything which I had seen before. There were more traces, too, of a physical organization, especially two vast, shadowy, circular plates upon either side, which may have been eyes, and a perfectly solid white projection between them which was as curved and cruel as the beak of a vulture.

"The whole aspect of this monster was formidable and threatening, and it kept changing its color from a very light mauve to a dark, angry purple so thick that it cast a shadow as it drifted between my monoplane and the sun. On the curve of its huge body there were three great projections which I can only describe as enormous bubbles, and I was convinced as I looked at them that they were charged with some extremely light gas which served to buoy up the misshapen and semi-solid mass in the rarefied air. The creature moved swiftly along, keeping pace easily with the monoplane, and for twenty miles or more it formed my horrible escort, hovering over me like a bird of prey which is waiting to pounce. Its method of progression—done so swiftly that it was not easy to follow—was to throw out a long, glutinous streamer in front of it, which in turn seemed to draw forward the rest of the writhing body. So elastic and gelatinous was it that never for two successive minutes was it the same shape, and yet each change made it more threatening and loathsome than the last.

"I knew that it meant mischief. Every purple flush of its hideous body told me so. The vague, goggling eyes which were turned always upon me were cold and merciless in their viscid hatred. I dipped the nose of my monoplane downwards to escape it. As I did so, as quick as a flash there shot out a long tentacle from this mass of floating blubber, and it fell as light and sinuous as a whip-lash across the front of my machine. There was a loud hiss as it lay for a moment across the hot engine, and it whisked itself into the air again, while the huge, flat body drew itself together as if in sudden pain. I dipped to a vol-piqué, but again a tentacle fell over the monoplane and was shorn off by the propeller as easily as it might have cut through a smoke wreath. A long, gliding, sticky, serpent-like coil came from behind and caught me round the waist, dragging me out of the fuselage. I tore at it, my fingers sinking into the smooth, glue-like surface, and for an instant I disengaged myself, but only to be caught round the boot by another coil, which gave me a jerk that tilted me almost on to my back.

"As I fell over I blazed off both barrels of my gun, though, indeed, it was like attacking an elephant with a pea-shooter to imagine that any human weapon could cripple that mighty bulk. And yet I aimed better than I knew, for, with a loud report, one of the great blisters upon the creature's back exploded with the puncture of the buck-shot. It was very clear that my conjecture was right, and that these vast, clear bladders were distended with some lifting gas, for in an instant the huge, cloud-like body turned sideways, desperately to find its balance, while the white beak snapped and gaped in horrible fury. But already I had shot away on the steepest glide that I dared to attempt, my engine still full on, the flying propeller and the force of gravity shooting me downwards like an aerolite. Far behind me I saw a dull, purplish smudge growing swiftly smaller and merging into the blue sky behind it. I was safe out of the deadly jungle of the outer air.

"Once out of danger I throttled my engine, for nothing tears a machine to pieces quicker than running on full power from a height. It was a glorious, spiral vol-plané from nearly eight miles of altitude—first, to the level of the silver cloud-bank, then to that of the storm-cloud beneath it, and finally, in beating rain, to the surface of the earth. I saw the Bristol Channel beneath me as I broke from the clouds, but, having still some petrol in my tank, I got twenty miles inland before I found myself stranded in a field half a mile from the village of Ashcombe. There I got three tins of petrol from a passing motor-car, and at ten minutes past six that evening I alighted gently in my own home meadow at Devizes, after such a journey as no mortal upon earth has ever yet taken and lived to tell the tale. I have seen the beauty and I have seen the horror of the heights—and greater beauty or greater horror than that is not within the ken of man.

"And now it is my plan to go once again before I give my results to the world. My reason for this is that I must surely have something to show by way of proof before I lay such a tale before my fellow-men. It is true that others will soon follow and will confirm what I have said, and yet I should wish to carry conviction from the first. Those lovely iridescent bubbles of the air should not be hard to capture. They drift slowly upon their way, and the swift monoplane could intercept their leisurely course. It is likely enough that they would dissolve in the heavier layers of the atmosphere, and that some small heap of amorphous jelly might be all that I should bring to earth with me. And yet something there would surely be by which I could substantiate my story. Yes, I will go, even if I run a risk by doing so. These purple horrors would not seem to be numerous. It is probable that I shall not see one. If I do I shall dive at once. At the worst there is always the shotgun and my knowledge of . . ."

Here a page of the manuscript is unfortunately missing. On the next page is written, in large, straggling writing:—

"Forty-three thousand feet. I shall never see earth again. They are beneath me, three of them. God help me; it is a dreadful death to die!"

Such in its entirety is the Joyce-Armstrong Statement. Of the man nothing has since been seen. Pieces of his shattered monoplane have been picked up in the preserves of Mr. Budd-Lushington upon the borders of Kent and Sussex, within a few miles of the spot where the notebook was discovered. If the unfortunate aviator's theory is correct that this air-jungle, as he called it, existed only over the south-west of England, then it would seem that he had fled from it at the full speed of his monoplane, but had been overtaken and devoured by these horrible creatures at some spot in the outer atmosphere above the place where the grim relics were found. The picture of that monoplane skimming down the sky, with the nameless terrors flying as swiftly beneath it and cutting it off always from the earth while they gradually closed in upon their victim, is one upon which a man who valued his sanity would prefer not to dwell. There are many, as I am aware, who still jeer at the facts which I have here set down, but even they must admit that Joyce-Armstrong has disappeared, and I could commend to them his own words: "This note-book may explain what I am trying to do, and how I lost my life in doing it. But no drivel about accidents or mysteries, if *you* please."

The Stone Ship
William Hope Hodgson

This story has an almost operatic grotesqueness and takes place in what may be one of the weirdest settings ever dreamed up. Needless to say, something horrible lives there.

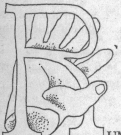RUM THINGS!—Of course there are
rum things happen at sea—As rum as ever there were. I
remember when I was in the *Alfred Jessop*, a small bar-
que, whose owner was her skipper, we came across a
most extraordinary thing.

We were twenty days out from London, and well down
into the tropics. It was before I took my ticket, and I was
in the fo'cas'le. The day had passed without a breath of
wind, and the night found us with all the lower sails up in
the buntlines.

Now, I want you to take good note of what I am going
to say:—

When it was dark in the second dog watch, there was
not a sail in sight; not even the far off smoke of a steamer,
and no land nearer than Africa, about a thousand miles
to the eastward of us.

It was our watch on deck from eight to twelve, midnight, and my look-out from eight to ten. For the first
hour, I walked to and fro across the break of the fo'cas'le
head, smoking my pipe and just listening to the quiet. . . .
Ever hear the kind of silence you can get away out at sea?

54

You need to be in one of the old-time windjammers, with all the lights dowsed, and the sea as calm and quiet as some queer plain of death. And then you want a pipe and the lonesomeness of the fo'cas'le head, with the caps'n to lean against while you listen and think. And all about you, stretching out into the miles, only and always the enormous silence of the sea, spreading out a thousand miles every way into the everlasting, brooding night. And not a light anywhere, out on all the waste of waters; nor ever a sound, as I have told, except the faint moaning of the masts and gear, as they chafe and whine a little to the occasional invisible roll of the ship.

And suddenly, across all this silence, I heard Jensen's voice from the head of the starboard steps, say:—

"Did you hear *that,* Duprey?"

"What?" I asked, cocking my head up. But as I questioned, I heard what he heard—the constant sound of running water, for all the world like the noise of a brook running down a hill-side. And the queer sound was surely not a hundred fathoms off our port bow!

"By gum!" said Jensen's voice, out of the darkness. "That's damned sort of funny!"

"Shut up!" I whispered, and went across, in my bare feet, to the port rail, where I leaned out into the darkness, and stared towards the curious sound.

The noise of a brook running down a hill-side continued, where there was no brook for a thousand sea-miles in any direction.

"What is it?" said Jensen's voice again, scarcely above a whisper now. From below him on the main-deck, there came several voices questioning:— "Hark!" "Stow the talk!" ". . . there!" "Listen!" "Lord love us, what is it?" . . . And then Jensen muttering to them to be quiet.

There followed a full minute, during which we all heard the brook, where no brook could ever run; and then, out of the night there came a sudden hoarse incredible sound:—oooaze, oooaze, arrr, arrr, oooaze—a stupendous sort of croak, deep and somehow abominable, out of the blackness. In the same instant, I found myself sniffing the air. There was a queer rank smell, stealing through the night.

"Forrard there on the look-out!" I heard the mate singing out, away aft. "Forrard there! What the blazes are you doing!"

I heard him come clattering down the port ladder from the poop, and then the sound of his feet at a run along the maindeck. Simultaneously, there was a thudding of bare feet, as the watch below came racing out of the fo'cas'le beneath me.

"Now then! Now then! Now then!" shouted the Mate, as he charged up on to the fo'cas'le head.

"What's up?"

"It's something off the port bow, Sir," I said. "Running water! And then that sort of howl.... Your night-glasses," I suggested.

"Can't see a thing," he growled, as he stared away through the dark. "There's a sort of mist. Phoo! what a devil of a stink!"

"Look!" said someone down on the main-deck. "What's that?"

I saw it in the same instant, and caught the Mate's elbow.

"Look, Sir," I said. "There's a light there, about three points off the bow. It's moving."

The Mate was staring through his night-glasses, and suddenly he thrust them into my hands:—

"See if you can make it out," he said, and forthwith put his hands round his mouth, and bellowed into the night:—"Ahoy there! Ahoy there! Ahoy there!" his voice going out lost into the silence and darkness all around. But there came never a comprehensible answer, only all the time the infernal noise of a brook running out there on the sea, a thousand miles from any brook of earth; and away on the port bow, a vague shapeless shining.

I put the glasses to my eyes, and stared. The light was bigger and brighter, seen through the binoculars; but I could make nothing of it, only a dull, elongated shining, that moved vaguely in the darkness, apparently a hundred fathoms or so, away on the sea.

"Ahoy there! Ahoy there!" sung out the Mate again. Then, to the men below:—"Quiet there on the main-deck!"

There followed about a minute of intense stillness, during which we all listened; but there was no sound, except the constant noise of water running steadily.

I was watching the curious shining, and I saw it flick out suddenly at the Mate's shout. Then in a moment I saw three dull lights, one under the other, that flicked in and out intermittently.

"Here, give me the glasses!" said the Mate, and grabbed them from me.

He stared intensely for a moment; then swore, and turned to me:—

"What do you make of them?" he asked, abruptly.

"I don't know, Sir," I said. "I'm just puzzled. Perhaps it's electricity, or something of that sort."

"Oh hell!" he replied, and leant far out over the rail, staring, "Lord!" he said, for the second time, "what a stink!"

As he spoke, there came a most extraordinary thing; for there sounded a series of heavy reports out of the darkness, seeming in the silence, almost as loud as the sound of small cannon.

"They're shooting!" shouted a man on the main-deck, suddenly.

The Mate said nothing; only he sniffed violently at the night air. "By Gum!" he muttered, "what is it?"

I put my hand over my nose; for there was a terrible, charnel-like stench filling all the night about us.

"Take my glasses, Duprey," said the Mate, after a few minutes further watching. "Keep an eye over yonder. I'm going to call the Captain."

He pushed his way down the ladder, and hurried aft. About five minutes later, he returned forrard with the

Captain and the Second and Third Mates, all in their shirts and trousers.

"Anything fresh, Duprey?" asked the Mate.

"No, Sir," I said, and handed him back his glasses. "The lights have gone again, and I think the mist is thicker. There's still the sound of running water out there."

The Captain and the three Mates stood some time along the port rail of the fo'cas'le head, watching through their night-glasses, and listening. Twice the Mate hailed; but there came no reply.

There was some talk, among the officers; and I gathered that the Captain was thinking of investigating.

"Clear one of the life-boats, Mr. Gelt," he said, at last. "The glass is steady; there'll be no wind for hours yet. Pick out a half a dozen men. Take 'em out of either watch, if they want to come. I'll be back when I've got my coat."

"Away aft with you, Duprey, and some of you others," said the Mate. "Get the cover off the port life-boat, and bail her out."

" 'I, 'i, Sir," I answered, and went away aft with the others.

We had the boat into the water within twenty minutes, which is good time for a wind-jammer, where boats are generally used as storage receptacles for odd-gear.

I was one of the men told off to the boat, with two others from our watch, and one from the starboard.

The Captain came down the end of the main tops'l halyards into the boat, and the Third after him. The Third took the tiller, and gave orders to cast off.

We pulled out clear of our vessel, and the Skipper told us to lie on our oars for a moment while he took his bearings. He leant forward to listen, and we all did the same. The sound of the running water was quite distinct across the quietness; but it struck me as seeming not so loud as earlier.

I remember now, that I noticed how plain the mist had become—a sort of warm, wet mist; not a bit thick; but just enough to make the night very dark, and to be visible, eddying slowly in a thin vapor round the port sidelight, looking like a red cloudiness swirling lazily through the red glow of the big lamp.

There was no other sound at this time, beyond the sound of the running water; and the Captain, after handing something to the Third Mate, gave the order to give-way.

I was rowing stroke, and close to the officers, and so was able to see dimly that the Captain had passed a heavy revolver over to the Third Mate.

"Ho!" I thought to myself, "so the Old Man's a notion there's really something dangerous over there."

I slipped a hand quickly behind me, and felt that my sheath knife was clear.

We pulled easily for about three or four minutes, with the sound of the water growing plainer somewhere ahead in the darkness; and astern of us, a vague red glowing through the night and vapor, showed where our vessel was lying.

We were rowing easily, when suddenly the bow-oar muttered "G'lord!" Immediately afterwards, there was a loud splashing in the water on his side of the boat.

"What's wrong in the bows, there?" asked the Skipper, sharply.

"There's somethin' in the water, Sir, messing round my oar," said the man.

I stopped rowing, and looked round. All the men did the same. There was a further sound of splashing, and the water was driven right over the boat in showers. Then the bow-oar called out:— "There's somethin' got a holt of my oar, Sir!"

I could tell the man was frightened; and I knew suddenly that a curious nervousness had come to me—a vague, uncomfortable dread, such as the memory of an ugly tale will bring, in a lonesome place. I believe every man in the boat had a similar feeling. It seemed to me in that moment, that a definite, muggy sort of silence was all round us, and this in spite of the sound of the splashing, and the strange noise of the running water somewhere ahead of us on the dark sea.

"It's let go the oar, Sir!" said the man.

Abruptly, as he spoke, there came the Captain's voice in a roar:—"Back water all!" he shouted. "Put some beef into it now! Back all! Back all! . . . Why the devil was no lantern put in the boat! Back now! Back! Back!"

We backed fiercely, with a will; for it was plain that the Old Man had some good reason to get the boat away pretty quickly. He was right, too; though, whether it was guess-work, or some kind of instinct that made him shout out at that moment, I don't know; only I am sure he could not have seen anything in that absolute darkness.

As I was saying, he was right in shouting to us to back; for we had not backed more than half a dozen fathoms, when there was a tremendous splash right ahead of us, as if a house had fallen into the sea; and a regular wave of sea-water came at us out of the darkness, throwing our bows up, and soaking us fore and aft.

"Good Lord!" I heard the Third Mate gasp out. "What the devil's that?"

"Back all! Back! Back!" the Captain sung out again.

After some moments, he had the tiller put over, and told us to pull. We gave way with a will, as you may think, and in a few minutes were alongside our own ship again.

"Now then, men," the Captain said, when we were safe aboard, "I'll not order any of you to come; but after the steward's served out a tot of grog each, those who are willing, can come with me, and we'll have another go at finding out what devil's work is going on over yonder."

He turned to the Mate, who had been asking questions:—

"Say, Mister," he said, "it's no sort of thing to let the boat go without a lamp aboard. Send a couple of the lads into the lamp locker, and pass out a couple of the anchor-lights, and that deck bull's-eye you use at nights for clearing up the ropes."

He whipped round on the Third:—"Tell the steward to buck up with that grog, Mr. Andrews," he said, "and while you're there, pass out the axes from the rack in my cabin."

The grog came along a minute later; and then the Third Mate with three big axes from out the cabin rack.

"Now then, men," said the Skipper, as we took our tots off, "those who are coming with me, had better take an axe each from the Third Mate. They're mighty good weapons in any sort of trouble."

We all stepped forward, and he burst out laughing, slapping his thigh.

"That's the kind of thing I like!" he said. "Mr. Andrews, the axes won't go round. Pass out that old cutlass from the steward's pantry. It's a pretty hefty piece of iron!"

The old cutlass was brought, and the man who was short of an axe collared it. By this time, two of the 'prentices had filled (at least we supposed they had filled them!) two of the ship's anchor-lights; also they had brought out the bull's-eye lamp we used when clearing up the ropes on a dark night. With the lights and the axes and the cutlass, we felt ready to face anything, and down we went again into the boat, with the Captain and the Third Mate after us.

"Lash one of the lamps to one of the boat-hooks, and rig it over the bows," ordered the Captain.

This was done, and in this way the light lit up the water for a couple of fathoms ahead of the boat; and made us feel less that something could come at us without our knowing. Then the painter was cast off, and we gave way again toward the sound of the running water, out there in the darkness.

I remember now that it struck me that our vessel had drifted a bit; for the sounds seemed farther away. The second anchor-light had been put in the stern of the boat, and the Third Mate kept it between his feet, while he steered. The Captain had the bull's-eye in his hand, and was pricking up the wick with his pocket-knife.

As we pulled, I took a glance or two over my shoulder; but could see nothing, except the lamp making a yellow halo in the mist round the boat's bows, as we forged ahead. Astern of us, on our quarter, I could see the dull red glow of our vessel's port light. That was all, and not a sound in all the sea, as you might say, except the roll of our oars in the rowlocks, and somewhere in the darkness ahead, that curious noise of water running steadily; now sounding, as I have said, fainter and seeming farther away.

"It's got my oar again, Sir!" exclaimed the man at the bow oar, suddenly, and jumped to his feet. He hove his oar up with a great splashing of water, into the air, and immediately something whirled and beat about in the yellow halo of light over the bows of the boat. There was a crash of breaking wood, and the boat-hook was broken. The lamp soused down into the sea, and was lost. Then in the darkness, there was a heavy splash, and a shout from the bow-oar:—"It's gone, Sir. It's loosed off the oar!"

"Vast pulling, all!" sung out the Skipper. Not that the order was necessary; for not a man was pulling. He had jumped up, and whipped a big revolver out of his coat pocket.

He had this in his right hand, and the bull's-eye in his left. He stepped forrard smartly over the oars from thwart to thwart, till he reached the bows, where he shone his light down into the water.

"My word!" he said. "Lord in Heaven! Saw anyone ever the like!"

And I doubt whether any man ever did see what we saw then; for the water was thick and living for yards round the boat with the hugest eels I ever saw before or after.

"Give way, Men," said the Skipper, after a minute. "Yon's no explanation of the almighty queer sounds out yonder we're hearing this night. Give way, lads!"

He stood right up in the bows of the boat, shining his bull's-eye from side to side, and flashing it down on the water.

"Give way, lads!" he said again. "They don't like the light, that'll keep them from the oars. Give way steady now. Mr. Andrews, keep her dead on for the noise out yonder."

We pulled for some minutes, during which I felt my oar plucked at twice; but a flash of the Captain's lamp seemed sufficient to make the brutes loose hold.

The noise of the water running appeared now quite near-sounding. About this time, I had a sense again of an added sort of silence to all the natural quietness of the sea. And I had a return of the curious nervousness that had touched me before. I kept listening intensely, as if I expected to hear some other sound than the noise of the water. It came to me suddenly that I had the kind of feeling one has in the aisle of a large cathedral. There was a sort of echo in the night—an incredibly faint reduplicating of the noise of our oars.

"Hark!" I said, audibly; not realizing at first that I was speaking aloud. "There's an echo—"

"That's it!" the Captain cut in, sharply. "I thought I heard something rummy!"

. . . "I thought I heard something rummy," said a thin ghostly echo, out of the night. . . "thought I heard something rummy" . . . "heard something rummy." The words went muttering and whispering to and fro in the night about us, in a rather a horrible fashion.

"Good Lord!" said the Old Man, in a whisper.

We had all stopped rowing, and were staring about us into the thin mist that filled the night. The Skipper was standing with the bull's-eye lamp held over his head, circling the beam of light round from port to starboard, and back again.

Abruptly, as he did so, it came to me that the mist was thinner. The sound of the running water was very near; but it gave back no echo.

"The water doesn't echo, Sir," I said. "That's damn funny!"

"That's damn funny," came back at me, from the darkness to port and starboard, in a multitudinous muttering. . . . "Damn funny! . . . funny . . . eey!"

"Give way!" said the Old Man, loudly. "I'll bottom this!"

"I'll bottom this. . . . Bottom this . . . this!" The echo came back in a veritable rolling of unexpected sound. And then we had dipped our oars again, and the night was full of the reiterated rolling echoes of our rowlocks.

Suddenly the echoes ceased, and there was, strangely, the sense of a great space about us, and in the same moment the sound of the water running appeared to be directly before us, but somehow up in the air.

"Vast rowing!" said the Captain, and we lay on our oars, staring round into the darkness ahead. The Old Man swung the beam of his lamp upwards, making circles with it in the night, and abruptly I saw something looming vaguely through the thinner-seeming mist.

"Look, Sir," I called to the Captain. "Quick, Sir, your light right above you! There's something up there!"

The Old Man flashed his lamp upwards, and found the thing I had seen. But it was too indistinct to make anything of, and even as he saw it, the darkness and mist seemed to wrap it about.

"Pull a couple of strokes, all!" said the Captain. "Stow your talk, there in the boat! . . . Again! . . . That'll do! Vast pulling!"

He was sending the beam of his lamp constantly across that part of the night where we had seen the thing, and suddenly I saw it again.

"There, Sir!" I said. "A little starboard with the light."

He flicked the light swiftly to the right, and immediately we all saw the thing plainly—a strangely-made mast, standing up there out of the mist, and looking like no spar I had ever seen.

It seemed now that the mist must lie pretty low on the

sea in places; for the mast stood up out of it plainly for several fathoms; but, lower, it was hidden in the mist, which, I thought, seemed heavier now all round us; but thinner, as I have said, above.

"Ship ahoy!" sung out the Skipper, suddenly. "Ship ahoy, there!" But for some moments there came never a sound back to us except the constant noise of the water running, not a score yards away; and then, it seemed to me that a vague echo beat back at us out of the mist, oddly:—"Ahoy! Ahoy! Ahoy!"

"There's something hailing us, Sir," said the Third Mate.

Now, that "something" was significant. It showed the sort of feeling that was on us all.

"That's na ship's mast as ever I've seen!" I heard the man next to me mutter. "It's got a unnatcheral look."

"Ahoy there!" shouted the Skipper again, at the top of his voice. "Ahoy there!"

With the suddenness of a clap of thunder there burst out at us a vast grunting:—oooaze; arrr; arrr; oooaze—a volume of sound so great that it seemed to make the loom of the oar in my hand vibrate.

"Good Lord!" said the Captain, and levelled his revolver into the mist; but he did not fire.

I had loosed one hand from my oar, and gripped my axe. I remember thinking that the Skipper's pistol wouldn't be much use against whatever thing made a noise like that.

"It wasn't ahead, Sir," said the Third Mate, abruptly, from where he sat and steered. "I think it came from somewhere over to starboard."

"Damn this mist!" said the Skipper. "Damn it! What a devil of a stink! Pass that other anchor-light forrard."

I reached for the lamp, and handed it to the next man, who passed it on.

"The other boat-hook," said the Skipper; and when he'd got it, he lashed the lamp to the hook end, and then lashed the whole arrangement upright in the bows, so that the lamp was well above his head.

"Now," he said. "Give way gently! And stand by to back-water, if I tell you. . . . Watch my hand, Mister," he added to the Third Mate. "Steer as I tell you."

We rowed a dozen slow strokes, and with every stroke, I took a look over my shoulder. The Captain was leaning forward under the big lamp, with the bull's-eye in one hand and his revolver in the other. He kept flashing the beam of the lantern up into the night.

"Good Lord!" he said, suddenly. "Vast pulling."

We stopped, and I slewed round on the thwart, and stared.

He was standing up under the glow of the anchor-light, and shining the bull's-eye up at a great mass that loomed dully through the mist. As he flicked the light to and fro over the great bulk, I realized that the boat was within some three or four fathoms of the hull of a vessel.

"Pull another stroke," the Skipper said, in a quiet voice, after a few minutes of silence. "Gently now! Gently! . . . Vast pulling!"

I slewed round again on my thwart and stared. I could see part of the thing quite distinctly now, and more of it, as I followed the beam of the Captain's lantern. She was a vessel right enough; but such a vessel as I had never seen. She was extraordinarily high out of the water, and seemed very short, and rose up into a queer mass at one end. But what puzzled me more, I think, than anything else, was the queer look of her sides, down which water was streaming all the time.

"That explains the sound of the water running," I thought to myself; "but what on earth is she built of?"

You will understand a little of my bewildered feelings, when I tell you that as the beam of the Captain's lamp shone on the side of this queer vessel, it showed stone everywhere—as if she were built out of stone. I never felt so dumb-founded in my life.

"She's stone, Cap'n" I said. "Look at her, Sir!"

I realised, as I spoke, a certain horribleness, of the un-natural. . . . A stone ship, floating out there in the night in the midst of the lonely Atlantic!

"She's stone," I said again, in that absurd way in which one reiterates, when one is bewildered.

"Look at the slime on her!" muttered the man next but one forrard of me. "She's a proper Davy Jones ship. By gum! she stinks like a corpse!"

"Ship ahoy!" roared the Skipper, at the top of his voice. "Ship ahoy! Ship ahoy!"

His shout beat back at us, in a curious, dank, yet metal-lic, echo, something the way one's voice sounds in an old disused quarry.

"There's no one aboard there, Sir," said the Third Mate. "Shall I put the boat alongside?"

"Yes, shove her up, Mister," said the Old Man. "I'll bottom this business. Pull a couple of strokes, aft there! In bow, and stand by to fend off."

The Third Mate laid the boat alongside, and we un-shipped our oars.

Then, I leant forward over the side of the boat, and pressed the flat of my hand upon the stark side of the ship. The water that ran down her side, sprayed out over my hand and wrist in a cataract; but I did not think about being wet, for my hand was pressed solid upon stone. . . . I pulled my hand back with a queer feeling.

"She's stone, right enough, Sir," I said to the Captain.

"We'll soon see what she is," he said. "Shove your oar up against her side, and shin up. We'll pass the lamp up to you as soon as you're aboard. Shove your axe in the back of your belt. I'll cover you with my gun, till you're aboard."

" 'I, 'i, Sir," I said; though I felt a bit funny at the thought of having to be the first aboard that damn rummy craft.

I put my oar upright against her side, and took a spring up from the thwart, and in a moment I was grabbing over my head for her rail, with every rag of me soaked through with the water that was streaming down her, and spraying out over the oar and me.

I got a firm grip of the rail, and hoisted my head high enough to look over; but I could see nothing. . . . what with the darkness, and the water in my eyes.

I knew it was no time for going slow, if there were danger aboard; so I went in over that rail in one spring, my boots coming down with a horrible, ringing, hollow, stony sound on her decks. I whipped the water out of my eyes and the axe out of my belt, all in the same moment; then I took a good stare fore and aft; but it was too dark to see anything.

"Come along, Duprey!" shouted the Skipper. "Collar the lamp."

I leant out sideways over the rail, and grabbed for the lamp with my left hand, keeping the axe ready in my right, and staring inboard; for I tell you, I was just mortally afraid in that moment of what might be aboard of her.

I felt the lamp-ring with my left hand, and gripped it. Then I switched it aboard, and turned fair and square to see where I'd gotten.

Now, you never saw such a packet as that, not in a hundred years, nor yet two hundred, I should think. She'd got a rum little main-deck, about forty feet long, and then came a step about two feet high, and another bit of a deck, with a little house on it.

That was the after end of her; and more I couldn't see, because the light of my lamp went no fatther, except to show me vaguely the big, cocked-up stern of her, going up into the darkness. I never saw a vessel made like her; not even in an old picture of old-time ships.

Forrard of me, was her mast—a big lump of a stick it was too, for her size. And here was another amazing thing, the mast of her looked just solid stone.

"Funny, isn't she, Duprey?" said the Skipper's voice at my back, and I came round on him with a jump.

"Yes," I said. "I'm puzzled. Aren't you, Sir?"

"Well," he said, "I am. If we were like the shellbacks they talk of in books, we'd be crossing ourselves. But, personally, give me a good heavy Colt, or the hefty chunk of steel you're cuddling."

He turned from me, and put his head over the rail.

"Pass up the painter, Jules," he said, to the bow-oar. Then to the Third Mate:—

"Bring 'em all up, Mister. If there's going to be anything rummy, we may as well make a picnic party of the lot. . . . Hitch that painter round the cleet yonder, Duprey," he added to me. "It looks good solid stone! . . . that's right. Come along."

He swung the thin beam of his lantern fore and aft, and then forrard again.

"Lord!" he said. "Look at that mast. It's stone. Give it a whack with the back of your axe, man; only remember she's apparently a bit of an old-timer! So go gently."

I took my axe short, and tapped the mast, and it rang dull, and solid, like a stone pillar, I struck it again, harder, and a sharp flake of stone flew past my cheek. The Skipper thrust his lantern close up to where I'd struck the mast.

"By George," he said, "she's absolute a stone ship—solid stone, afloat here out of Eternity, in the middle of the wide Atlantic. . . . Why! She must weigh a thousand tons more than she's buoyancy to carry. It's just impossible. . . . It's—"

He turned his head quickly, at a sound in the darkness along the decks. He flashed his light that way, across the after decks; but we could see nothing.

"Get a move on you in the boat!" he said sharply, stepping to the rail and looking down. "For once I'd really prefer a little more of your company. . . ." He came round like a flash. "Duprey, what was that?" he asked in a low voice.

"I certainly heard something, Sir," I said. "I wish the others would hurry. By Jove! Look! What's that—"

"Where?" he said, and sent the beam of his lamp to where I pointed with my axe.

"There's nothing," he said, after circling the light all over the deck. "Don't go imagining things. There's enough solid unnatural fact here, without trying to add to it."

There came the splash and thud of feet behind, as the first of the men came up over the side, and jumped clumsily into the lee scuppers, which had water in them. You see she had a cant to that side, and I supposed the water had collected there.

The rest of the men followed, and then the Third Mate. That made six men of us, all well armed; and I felt a bit more comfortable, as you can think.

"Hold up that lamp of yours, Duprey, and lead the way," said the Skipper. "You're getting the post of honor this trip!"

" 'I, 'i, Sir," I said, and stepped forward, holding up the lamp in my left hand, and carrying my axe half way down the haft, in my right.

"We'll try aft, first," said the Captain, and led the way himself, flashing the bull's-eye to and fro. At the raised portion of the deck, he stopped.

"Now," he said, in his queer way, "let's have a look at this. . . . Tap it with your axe, Duprey. . . . Ah!" he added, as I hit it with the back of my axe. "That's what we call stone at home, right enough. She's just as rum as anything I've seen while I've been fishing. We'll go on aft and have a peep into the deck-house. Keep your axes handy, men."

We walked slowly up to the curious little house, the deck rising to it with quite a slope. At the foreside of the little deck-house, the Captain pulled up, and shone his bull's-eye down at the deck. I saw that he was looking at what was plainly the stump of the after mast. He stepped closer to it, and kicked it with his foot; and it gave out the same dull, solid note that the foremast had done. It was obviously a chunk of stone.

I held up my lamp so that I could see the upper part of the house more clearly. The fore-part had two square window-spaces in it; but there was no glass in either of them; and the blank darkness within the queer little place, just seemed to stare out at us.

And then I saw something suddenly ... a great shaggy head of red hair was rising slowly into sight, through the port window, the one nearest to us.

"My God! What's that, Cap'n?" I called out. But it was gone, even as I spoke.

"What?" he asked, jumping at the way I had sung out.

"At the port window, Sir," I said. "A great red-haired head. It came right up to the window-place; and then it went in a moment.

The Skipper stepped right up to the little dark window, and pushed his lantern through into the blackness. He flashed a light round; then withdrew the lantern.

"Bosh, man!" he said. "That's twice you've got fancying things. Ease up your nerves a bit!"

"I did see it!" I said, almost angrily. "It was like a great red-haired head. . . ."

"Stow it, Duprey!" he said, though not sneeringly. "The house is absolutely empty. Come round to the door, if the Infernal Masons that built her went in for doors! Then you'll see for yourself. All the same, keep your axes ready, lads. I've a notion there's something pretty queer aboard here."

We went up round the after-end of the little house, and here we saw what appeared to be a door.

The Skipper felt at the queer, odd-shapen handle, and pushed at the door; but it had stuck fast.

"Here, one of you!" he said, stepping back. "Have a whack at this with your axe. Better use the back."

One of the men stepped forward, and I stood away to give him room. As his axe struck, the door went to pieces with exactly the same sound that a thin slab of stone would make, when broken.

"Stone!" I heard the Captain mutter, under his breath. "By Gum! What is she?"

I did not wait for the Skipper. He had put me a bit of edge, and I stepped bang in through the open doorway, with the lamp high, and holding my axe short and ready; but there was nothing in the place, save a stone seat running all round, except where the doorway opened on to the deck.

"Find your red-haired monster?" asked the Skipper, at my elbow.

I said nothing. I was suddenly aware that he was all on the jump with some inexplicable fear. I saw his glance going everywhere about him. And then his eye caught mine, and he saw that I realised. He was a man almost callous to fear, that is the fear of danger in what I might call any normal sea-faring shape. And this palpable nerviness affected me tremendously. He was obviously doing his best to throttle it; and trying all he knew to hide it. I had a sudden warmth of understanding for him, and dreaded lest the men should realise his state. Funny that I should be able at that moment to be aware of anything but my own bewildered fear and expectancy of intruding upon something monstrous at any instant. Yet I describe exactly my feelings, as I stood there in the house.

"Shall we try below, Sir?" I said, and turned to where a flight of stone steps led down into an utter blackness, out which rose a strange, dank scent of the sea ... an imponderable mixture of brine and darkness.

"The worthy Duprey leads the van!" said the Skipper; but I felt no irritation now. I knew that he must cover his fright, until he had got control again; and I think he felt, somehow, that I was backing him up. I remember now that I went down those stairs into that unknowable and ancient cabin, as much aware in that moment of the Captain's state, as of that extraordinary thing I had just seen at the little window, or of my own half-funk of what we might see any moment.

The Captain was at my shoulder, as I went, and behind

him came the Third Mate, and then the men, all in single file; for the stairs were narrow.

I counted seven steps down, and then my foot splashed into water on the eighth. I held the lamp low and stared. I had caught no glimpse of a reflection, and I saw now that this was owing to a curious, dull, greyish scum that lay thinly on the water, seeming to match the color of the stone which composed the steps and bulk-heads.

"Stop!" I said. "I'm in water!"

I let my foot down slowly, and got the next step. Then sounded with my axe, and found the floor at the bottom. I stepped down and stood up to my thighs in water.

"It's all right, Sir," I said, suddenly whispering. I held my lamp up, and glanced quickly about me.

"It's not deep. There's two doors here. . . ."

I whirled my axe up as I spoke; for suddenly, I had realised that one of the doors was open a little. It seemed to move, as I stared, and I could have imagined that a vague undulation ran towards me, across the dull-scum-covered water.

"The door's opening!" I said, aloud, with a sudden sick feeling. "Look out!"

I backed from the door, staring; but nothing came. And abruptly, I had control of myself; for I realised that the door was not moving. It had not moved at all. It was simply ajar.

"It's all right, sir," I said. "It's not opening."

I stepped forward again a pace towards the doors, as the Skipper and the Third Mate came down with a jump, splashing water all over me.

The Captain still had the "nerves" on him, as I think I could feel, even then; but he hid it well.

"Try the door, Mister. I've jumped my damn lamp out!" he growled to the Third Mate; who pushed at the door on my right; but it would not open beyond the nine or ten inches it was fixed ajar.

"There's this one here, Sir," I whispered, and held my lantern up to the closed door that lay on my left.

"Try it," said the Skipper, in an undertone. We did so, but it also was fixed. I whirled my axe suddenly, and struck the door heavily in the center of the main panel, and the whole thing crashed into flinders of stone, that went with hollow sounding splashes into the darkness beyond.

"Goodness!" said the Skipper, in a startled voice; for my action had been so instant and unexpected. He covered his lapse, in a moment, by the warning:——

"Look out for bad air!" But I was already inside with the lamp, and holding my axe handily. There was no bad air; for right across from me was a split clean through the ship's side, that I could have put my two arms through, just above the level of the scummy water.

The place I had broken into was a cabin, of a kind; but seemed strange and dank, and too narrow to breathe in; and wherever I turned, I saw stone. The Third Mate and the Skipper gave simultaneous expressions of disgust at the wet dismalness of the place.

"It's all of stone," I said, and brought my axe hard against the front of a sort of squat cabinet, which was built into the after bulk-heads. It caved in, with a crash of splintered stone.

"Empty!" I said, and turned instantly away.

The Skipper and the Third Mate, with the men who were now peering in at the door, crowded out; and in that moment, I pushed my axe under my arm, and thrust my hand into the burst stone-chest. Twice I did this, with almost the speed of lightning, and shoved what I had seen into the side-pocket of my coat. Then, I was following the others; and not one of them had noticed a thing. As for me, I was quivering with excitement, so that my knees shook; for I had caught the unmistakable gleam of gems; and had grabbed for them in that one swift instant.

I wonder whether anyone can realise what I felt in that moment. I knew that, if my guess were right, I had snatched the power in that one miraculous moment, that would lift me from the weary life of a common shellback, to the life of ease that had been mine during my early years. I tell you, in that instant, as I staggered almost blindly out of that dark little apartment, I had no thought of any horror that might be held in that incredible vessel, out there afloat on the wide Atlantic.

I was full of one blinding thought, that possibly I was *rich!* And I wanted to get somewhere by myself as soon as possible, to see whether I was right. Also, if I could, I meant to get back to that strange cabinet of stone, if the chance came; for I knew that the two handfuls I had grabbed had left a lot behind.

Only, whatever I did, I must let no one guess; for then I should probably lose everything, or have but an infinitesimal share doled out to me, of the wealth that I believed to be in those glittering things there in the sidepocket of my coat.

I began immediately to wonder what other treasures there might be aboard; and then, abruptly, I realised that the Captain was speaking to me:—

"The light, Duprey, damn you!" he was saying, angrily, in a low tone. "What's the matter with you! Hold it up."

I pulled myself together, and shoved the lamp above my head. One of the men was swinging his axe, to beat in the door that seemed to have stood so eternally ajar; and the rest were standing back, to give him room. Crash! went the axe, and half the door fell inward, in a shower of broken stone, making dismal splashes in the darkness. The man struck again, and the rest of the door fell away, with a sullen slump into the water.

"The lamp," muttered the Captain. But I had hold of myself once more, and I was stepping forward slowly through the thigh-deep water, even before he spoke.

I went a couple of paces in through the black gape of the doorway, and then stopped and held the lamp so as to get a view of the place. As I did so, I remember how the intense silence struck home on me. Every man of us must surely have been holding his breath; and there must have been some heavy quality, either in the water, or in the scum that floated on it, that kept it from rippling against the sides of the bulkheads, with the movements we had made.

At first, as I held the lamp (which was burning badly), I could not get its position right to show me anything, except that I was in a very large cabin for so small a vessel. Then I saw that a table ran along the center, and the top of it was no more than a few inches above the water. On each side of it, there rose the backs of what were evidently two rows of massive, olden looking chairs. At the far end of the table, there was a huge, immobile, humped something.

I stared at this for several moments; then I took three slow steps forward, and stopped again; for the thing resolved itself, under the light from the lamp, into the figure of an enormous man, seated at the end of the table, his face bowed forward upon his arms. I was amazed, and thrilling abruptly with new fears and vague impossible thoughts. Without moving a step, I held the light nearer at arm's length. . . . The man was of stone, like everything in that extraordinary ship.

"That foot!" said the Captain's voice, suddenly cracking. "Look at that foot!" His voice sounded amazingly startling and hollow in that silence, and the words seemed to come back sharply at me from the vaguely seen bulkheads.

I whipped my light to starboard, and saw what he meant—a huge human foot was sticking up out of the water, on the right hand of the table. It was enormous. I have never seen so vast a foot. And it also was of stone.

And then, as I stared, I saw that there was a great head above the water, over the bulkhead.

"I've gone mad!" I said, out loud, as I saw something else, more incredible.

"My God! Look at the hair on the head!" said the Captain. . . . It's growing!" he called out once more.

I was looking. On the great head, there was becoming

visible a huge mass of red hair, that was surely and unmistakably rising up, as we watched it.

"It's what I saw at the window!" I said. "It's what I saw at the window! I told you I saw it!"

"Come out of that, Duprey," said the Third Mate, quietly.

"Let's get out of here!" muttered one of the men. Two or three of them called out the same thing; and then, in a moment, they began a mad rush up the stairway.

I stood dumb, where I was. The hair rose up in a horrible living fashion on the great head, waving and moving. It rippled down over the forehead, and spread abruptly over the whole gargantuan stone face, hiding the features completely. Suddenly, I swore at the thing madly, and I hove my axe at it. Then I was backing crazily for the door, slumping the scum as high as the deck-beams, in my fierce haste. I reached the stairs, and caught at the stone rail, that was modelled like a rope; and so hove myself up out of the water. I reached the deck-house, where I had seen the great head of hair. I jumped through the doorway, out on to the decks, and felt the night air sweet on my face. . . . Goodness! I ran forward along the decks. There was a Babel of shouting in the waist of the ship, and a thudding of feet running. Some of the men were singing out, to get into the boat; but the Third Mate was shouting that they must wait for me.

"He's coming," called someone. And then I was among them.

"Turn that lamp up, you idiot," said the Captain's voice. "This is just where we want light!"

I glanced down, and realised that my lamp was almost out. I turned it up, and it flared, and began again to dwindle.

"Those damned boys never filled it," I said. "They deserve their necks breaking."

The men were literally tumbling over the side, and the Skipper was hurrying them.

"Down with you into the boat," he said to me. "Give me the lamp. I'll pass it down. Get a move on you!"

The Captain had evidently got his nerve back again. This was more like the man I knew. I handed him the lamp, and went over the side. All the rest had now gone, and the Third Mate was already in the stern, waiting.

As I landed on the thwart, there was a sudden strange noise from aboard the ship—a sound, as if some stone object were trundling down the sloping decks, from aft. In that one moment, I got what you might truly call the "horrors." I seemed suddenly able to believe incredible possibilities.

"The stone men!" I shouted. "Jump, Captain! Jump! Jump!" The vessel seemed to roll oddly.

Abruptly, the Captain yelled out something, that not one of us in the boat understood. There followed a succession of tremendous sounds, aboard the ship, and I saw his shadow swing out huge against the thin mist, as he turned suddenly with the lamp. He fired twice with his revolver.

"The hair!" I shouted. "Look at the hair!"

We all saw it—the great head of red hair that we had seen grow visibly on the monstrous stone head, below in the cabin. It rose above the rail, and there was a moment of intense stillness, in which I heard the Captain gasping. The Third Mate fired six times at the thing, and I found myself fixing an oar up against the side of that abominable vessel, to get aboard.

As I did so, there came one appalling crash, that shook the stone ship fore and aft, and she began to cant up, and my oar slipped and fell into the boat. Then the Captain's voice screamed something in a choking fashion above us. The ship lurched forward and paused. Then another crash came, and she rocked over towards us; then away from us again. The movement away from us continued, and the round of the vessel's bottom showed, vaguely. There was a smashing of glass above us, and the dim glow of light aboard vanished. Then the vessel fell clean from us, with a giant splash. A huge wave came at us, out of the night, and half filled the boat.

The boat nearly capsized, then righted and presently steadied.

"Captain!" shouted the Third Mate. "Captain!" But there came never a sound; only presently, out of all the night, a strange murmuring of waters.

"Captain!" he shouted once more; but his voice just went lost and remote into the darkness.

"She's foundered!" I said.

"Out oars," sung out the Third. "Put your backs into it. Don't stop to bail!"

For half an hour we circled the spot slowly. But the strange vessel had indeed foundered and gone down into the mystery of the deep sea, with her mysteries.

Finally we put about, and returned to the *Alfred Jessop*.

Now, I want you to realize that what I am telling you is a plain and simple tale of fact. This is no fairy tale, and I've not done yet; and I think this yarn should prove to you that some mighty strange things do happen at sea, and always will while the world lasts. It's the home of all mysteries; for it's the one place that is really difficult for humans to investigate. Now just listen:—

The Mate had kept the bell going, from time to time, and so we came back pretty quickly, having as we came, a strange repetition of the echoey reduplication of our oar-sounds; but we never spoke a word; for not one of us wanted to hear those beastly echoes again, after what we had just gone through. I think we all had a feeling that there was something a bit hellish aboard that night.

We got aboard, and the Third explained to the Mate what had happened; but he would hardly believe the yarn. However, there was nothing to do, but wait for daylight; so we were told to keep about the deck, and keep our eyes and ears open.

One thing the Mate did showed he was more impressed by our yarn than he would admit. He had all the ships' lanterns lashed up round the decks, to the sheerpoles; and he never told us to give up either the axes or cutlass.

It was while we were keeping about the decks, that I took the chance to have a look at what I had grabbed. I tell you, what I found made me nearly forget the Skipper, and all the rummy things that had happened. I had twenty-six stones in my pocket and four of them were diamonds, respectively 9, 11, 13½ and 17 carats in weight, uncut, that is. I know quite something about diamonds. I'm not going to tell you how I learnt what I know; but I would not have taken a thousand pounds for the four, as they lay there, in my hand. There was also a big, dull stone, that looked red inside. I'd have dumped it over the side, I thought so little of it; only, I argued that it must be something, or it would never have been among that lot. Lord! but I little knew what I'd got; not then. Why, the thing was as big as a fair-sized walnut. You may think it funny that I thought of the four diamonds first; but you see, I *know* diamonds when I see them. They're things I understand; but I never saw a ruby, in the rough, before or since. Good Lord! And to think I'd have thought nothing of heaving it over the side!

You see, a lot of the stones were not anything much; that is, not in the modern market. There were two big topazes, and several onyx and corelians—nothing much. There were five hammered slugs of gold about two ounces each they would be. And then a prize—one winking green devil of an emerald. You're got to know an emerald to look for the "eye" of it, in the rough; but it is there—the eye of some hidden devil staring up at you. Yes, I'd seen an emerald before, and I knew I held a lot of money in that one stone alone.

And then I remembered what I'd missed, and cursed myself for not grabbing a third time. But that feeling lasted only a moment. I thought of the beastly part that had been the Skipper's share; while there I stood safe under one of the lamps, with a fortune in my hands. And then, abruptly, as you can understand, my mind was filled with the crazy wonder and bewilderment of what had happened. I felt how absurdly ineffectual my imagination was to comprehend anything understandable out of it all, except that the Captain had certainly gone, and I had just as certainly had a piece of impossible luck.

Often, during that time of waiting, I stopped to take a look at the things I had in my pocket; always careful that no one about the decks should come near me, to see what I was looking at.

Suddenly the Mate's voice came sharp along the decks:—

"Call the doctor, one of you," he said. "Tell him to get the fire in and the coffee made."

" 'I, Sir," said one of the men; and I realized that the dawn was growing vaguely over the sea.

Half an hour later, the "doctor" shoved his head out of the galley doorway, and sung out that coffee was ready.

The watch below turned out, and had theirs with the watch on deck, all sitting along the spar that lay under the port rail.

As the daylight grew, we kept a constant watch over the side; but even now we could see nothing; for the thin mist still hung low on the sea.

"Hear that?" said one of the men, suddenly. And, indeed, the sound must have been plain for a half a mile round.

"Ooaaze, ooaaze, arr, arrrr, oooaze—"

"By George!" said Tallett, one of the other watch; "that's a beastly sort of thing to hear."

"Look!" I said. "What's that out yonder?"

The mist was thinning under the effect of the rising sun, and tremendous shapes seemed to stand towering half-seen, away to port. A few minutes passed, while we stared. Then, suddenly, we heard the Mate's voice—

"All hands on deck!" he was shouting, along the decks.

I ran aft a few steps.

"Both watches are out, Sir," I called.

"Very good!" said the Mate. "Keep handy all of you.

Some of you have got the axes. The rest had better take a caps-n-bar each, and stand-by till I find what this devilment is, out yonder."

" 'I, 'i Sir," I said, and turned forrard. But there was no need to pass on the Mate's orders; for the men had heard, and there was a rush for the capstanbars, which are a pretty hefty kind of cudgel, as any sailorman knows. We lined the rail again, and stared away to port.

"Look out, you sea-devvils," shouted Timothy Galt, a huge Irishman, waving his bar excitedly, and peering the rail into the mist, which was steadily thinning, as the day grew.

Abruptly there was a simultaneous cry—*"Rocks!"* shouted everyone.

I never saw such a sight. As at last the mist thinned, we could see them. All the sea to port was literally cut about with far-reaching reefs of rock. In places the reefs lay just submerged; but in others they rose into extraordinary and fantastic rock-spires, and arches, and islands of jagged rock.

"Jehosaphat!" I heard the Third Mate shout: "Look at that, Mister! Look at that! Lord! how did we take the boat through that, without stoving her!"

Everything was so still for the moment, with all the men just staring and amazed, that I could hear every word come along the decks.

"There's sure been a submarine earthquake somewhere," I heard the First Mate. "The bottom of the sea's just riz up here, quiet and gentle, during the night; and God's mercy we aren't now a-top of one of those ornaments out there."

And then, you know, I saw it all. Everything that had looked mad and impossible, began to be natural; though it was, none the less, all amazing and wonderful.

There had been during the night, a slow lifting of the sea-bottom, owing to some action of the Internal Pressures. The rocks had risen so gently that they had made never a sound; and the stone ship had risen with them out of the deep sea. She had evidently lain on one of the submerged reefs, and so had seemed to us to be just afloat in the sea. And she accounted for the water we heard running. She was naturally bung full, as you might say, and took longer to shed the water than she did to rise. She had probably some biggish holes in her bottom. I began to get my "soundings" a bit, as I might call it in sailor talk. The natural wonders of the sea beat all made-up yarns that ever were!

The Mate sung out to us to man the boat again, and told the Third Mate to take her out to where we lost the Skipper, and have a final look round, in case there might be any chance to find the Old Man's body anywhere about.

"Keep a man in the bows to look out for sunk rocks, Mister," the Mate told the Third, as we pulled off. "Go slow. There'll be no wind yet awhile. See if you can fix up what made those noises, while you're looking round."

We pulled right across about thirty fathoms of clear water, and in a minute we were between two great arches of rock. It was then I realized that the reduplicating of our oar-roll was the echo from these on each side of us. Even in the sunlight, it was queer to hear again that same strange cathedral echoey sound that we had heard in the dark.

We passed under the huge arches, all hung with deep-sea slime. And presently we were heading straight for a gap, where two low reefs swept in to the apex of a huge horseshoe. We pulled for about three minutes, and then the Third gave the word to vast pulling.

"Take the boat-hook, Duprey," he said, "and go for-rard, and see we don't hit anything."

" 'I, 'i, Sir," I said, and drew in my oar.

"Give way again gently!" said the Third; and the boat moved forward for another thirty or forty yards.

"We're right on to a reef, Sir," I said, presently, as I stared down over the bows. I sounded with the boat-hook. "There's about three feet of water, Sir," I told him.

"Vast pulling," ordered the Third. "I reckon we are right over the rock, where we found that rum packet last night." He leant over the side, and stared down.

"There's a stone cannon on the rock, right under the bows of the boat," I said. Immediately afterwards I shouted—

"There's the hair, Sir! There's the hair! It's on the reef. There's two! There's three! There's one on the cannon!"

"All right! All right, Duprey! Keep cool," said the Third Mate. "I can see them. You've enough intelligence not to be superstitious now the whole thing's explained. They're some kind of big hairy sea-caterpillar. Prod one with your boat-hook."

I did so; a little ashamed of my sudden bewilderment. The thing whipped round like a tiger, at the boat-hook. It lapped itself round and round the boat-hook, while one hind portion of it kept gripped to the rock, and I could no more pull the boat-hook from its grip, than fly; though I pulled till I sweated.

"Take the point of your cutlass to it, Varley," said the Third Mate. "Jab it through."

The bow-oar did so, and the brute loosed the boat-hook, and curled up round a chunk of rock, looking like a great ball of red hair.

"Goodness!" I said. "That's what killed the Old Man—one of those things! Look at all those marks in the wood, where it's gripped it with about a hundred legs."

I drew the boat-hook up, and examined it.

I passed the boat-hook aft to the Third Mate to look at.

"They're about as dangerous as they can be, Sir, I reckon," I told him.

"Makes you think of African centipedes, only these are big and strong enough to kill an elephant, I should think."

"Don't lean all on one side of the boat!" shouted the Third Mate, as the men stared over. "Get back to your places. Give way, there! . . . Keep a good look-out for any signs of the ship or the Captain, Duprey."

For nearly an hour, we pulled to and fro over the reef; but we never saw either the stone ship or the Old Man again. The queer craft must have rolled off into the profound depths that lay on each side of the reef.

As I leant over the bows, staring down all that long while at the submerged rocks, I was able to understand almost everything, except the various extraordinary noises.

The cannon made it unmistakably clear that the ship which had been hove up from the sea-bottom, with the rising of the reef, had been originally a normal enough wooden vessel of a time far removed from our own. At the sea-bottom, she had evidently undergone some natural mineralizing process, and this explained her stony appearance. The stone men had been evidently humans who had been drowned in her cabin, and their swollen tissues had been subjected to the same natural process, which, however, had also deposited heavy encrustations upon them, so that their size, when compared with the normal, was prodigious.

The mystery of the hair, I had already discovered; but there remained, among other things, the tremendous bangs we had heard. These were, possibly, explained later, while we were making a final examination of the rocks to the westward, prior to returning to our ship. Here we discovered the burst and swollen bodies of several extraordinary deep-sea creatures, of the eel variety. They must have had a girth, in life, of many feet, and one that we measured roughly with an oar, must have been quite forty feet long. They had, apparently, burst on being lifted from the tremendous pressure of the deep sea, into the light air pressure above water, and hence might account for the loud reports we had heard; though, personally, I incline to think these loud bangs were more probably caused by the splitting of the rocks under new stresses.

As for the roaring sounds, I can only conclude that they were caused by a peculiar species of grampus-like fish, of enormous size, which we found dead and hugely distended on one of the rocky masses. This fish must have weighed at least four or five tons, and when prodded with a heavy oar, there came from its peculiar snout-shaped mouth, a low, hoarse sound, like a weak imitation of the tremendous sounds we had heard during the past night.

Regarding the apparently carved handrail, like a rope up the side of the cabin stairs, I realize that this had undoubtedly been actual rope at one time.

Recalling the heavy, trundling sounds aboard, just after I climbed down into the boat, I can only suppose that these were made by some stone object, possibly a fossilized gun-carriage, rolling down the decks, as the ship began to slip off the rocks, and bows sank lower in the water.

The varying lights must have been the strongly phosphorescent bodies of some of the deep-sea creatures, moving about on the upheaved reefs. As for the giant splash that occurred in the darkness ahead of the boat, this must have been due to some large portion of heaved-up rock, over-balancing and rolling back into the sea.

No one aboard ever learnt about the jewels. I took care of that! I sold the ruby badly, so I've heard since; but I do not grumble even now. Twenty-three thousand pounds I had for it alone, from a merchant in London. I learned afterwards he made double that on it; but I don't spoil my pleasure by grumbling. I wonder often how the stones and things came where I found them; but she carried guns, as I've told, I think: and there's rum doings happen at sea; yes, by George!

The smell—oh that I guess was due to heaving all that deep-sea slime up for human noses to smell at.

This yarn is, of course, known in nautical circles, and was briefly mentioned in the old *Nautical Mercury* of 1879. The series of volcanic reefs (which disappeared in 1883) were charted under the name of the "Alfred Jessop Shoals and Reefs"; being named after our Captain who discovered them and lost his life on them.

The Sea Was Wet As Wet Could Be

Gahan Wilson

Like any other anthologist who writes, I was unable to resist sneaking in one of my own creations. It belongs here, though, as it scared me when and as I wrote it, and it scares me now when I read it. I hope it has the same effect on you.

FELT WE MADE an embarrassing contrast to the open serenity of the scene around us. The pure blue of the sky was unmarked by a single cloud or bird, and nothing stirred on the vast stretch of beach except ourselves. The sea, sparkling under the freshness of the early morning sun, looked invitingly clean. I wanted to wade into it and wash myself, but I was afraid I would contaminate it.

We are a contamination here, I thought. We're like a group of sticky bugs crawling in an ugly little crowd over polished marble. If I were God and looked down and saw us, lugging our baskets and our silly, bright blankets, I would step on us and squash us with my foot.

We should have been lovers or monks in such a place, but we were only a crowd of bored and boring drunks. You were always drunk when you were with Carl. Good old, mean old Carl was the greatest little drink pourer in the world. He used drinks like other types of sadists use whips. He kept beating you with them until you dropped or sobbed or went mad, and he enjoyed every step of the process.

We'd been drinking all night, and when the morning came, somebody, I think it was Mandie, got the great idea that we should all go out on a picnic. Naturally, we thought it was an inspiration, we were nothing if not real sports, and so we'd packed some goodies, not forgetting the liquor, and we'd piled into the car, and there we were, weaving across the beach, looking for a place to spread our tacky banquet.

We located a broad, low rock, decided it would serve for our table, and loaded it with the latest in plastic chinaware, a haphazard collection of food and a quantity of bottles.

Someone had packed a tin of Spam among the other offerings and, when I saw it. I was suddenly overwhelmed with an absurd feeling of nostalgia. It reminded me of the war and of myself soldierboying up through Italy. It also reminded me of how long ago the whole thing had been and how little I'd done of what I'd dreamed I'd do back then.

I opened the Spam and sat down to be alone with it and my memories, but it wasn't to be for long. The kind of people who run with people like Carl don't like to be alone, ever, especially with their memories, and they can't imagine anyone else might, at least now and then, have a taste for it.

My rescuer was Irene. Irene was particularly sensitive about seeing people alone because being alone had several times nearly produced fatal results for her. Being alone and taking pills to end the being alone.

"What's wrong, Phil?" she asked.

"Nothing's wrong," I said, holding up a forkful of the pink Spam in the sunlight. "It tastes just like it always did. They haven't lost their touch."

She sat down on the sand beside me, very carefully, so as to avoid spilling the least drop of what must have been her millionth Scotch.

"Phil," she said, "I'm worried about Mandie. I really am. She looks so unhappy!"

I glanced over at Mandie. She had her head thrown back and she was laughing uproariously at some joke Carl had just made. Carl was smiling at her with his teeth glistening and his eyes deep down dead as ever.

"Why should Mandie be happy?" I asked. "What, in God's name, has she got to be happy about?"

"Oh, Phil," said Irene. "You pretend to be such an awful cynic. She's *alive,* isn't she?"

I looked at her and wondered what such a statement meant, coming from someone who'd tried to do herself in as earnestly and as frequently as Irene. I decided that I did not know and that I would probably never know. I also decided I didn't want anymore of the Spam. I turned to throw it away, doing my bit to litter up the beach, and then I saw them.

They were far away, barely bigger than two dots, but you could tell there was something odd about them even then.

"We've got company," I said.

Irene peered in the direction of my point.

"Look, everybody," she cried. "We've got company!"

Everybody looked, just as she had asked them to.

"What the hell is this?" asked Carl. "Don't they know this is my private property?" And then he laughed.

Carl had fantasies about owning things and having power. Now and then he got drunk enough to have little flashes of believing he was king of the world.

"You tell 'em, Carl!" said Horace.

Horace had sparkling quips like that for almost every occasion. He was tall and bald and he had a huge Adam's apple and, like myself, he worked for Carl. I would have felt sorrier for Horace than I did if I hadn't had a sneaky suspicion that he was really happier when groveling. He lifted one scrawny fist and shook it in the direction of the distant pair.

"You guys better beat it," he shouted. "This is private property!"

"Will you shut up and stop being such an ass?" Mandie asked him. "It's not polite to yell at strangers, dear, and this may damn well be *their* beach for all you know."

Mandie happens to be Horace's wife. Horace's children treat him about the same way. He busied himself with zipping up his windbreaker because it was getting cold and because he had received an order to be quiet.

I watched the two approaching figures. The one was tall and bulky, and he moved with a peculiar, swaying gait. The other was short and hunched into himself, and he walked in a fretful, zigzag line beside his towering companion.

"They're heading straight for us," I said.

The combination of the cool wind that had come up, and the approach of the two strangers, had put a damper on our little group. We sat quietly and watched them coming closer. The nearer they got, the odder they looked.

"For heaven's sake!" said Irene. "The little one's wearing a square hat!"

"I think it's made of paper," said Mandie, squinting. "Folded newspaper."

"Will you look at the mustache on the big bastard?" asked Carl. "I don't think I've ever seen a bigger bush in my life."

"They remind me of something," I said.

The others turned to look at me.

The Walrus and the Carpenter . . .

"They remind me of the Walrus and the Carpenter," I said.

"The who?" asked Mandie.

"Don't tell me you never heard of the Walrus and the Carpenter?" asked Carl.

"Never once," said Mandie.

"Disgusting," said Carl. "You're an uncultured bitch. The Walrus and the Carpenter are probably two of the most famous characters in literature. They're in a poem by Lewis Caroll in one of the Alice books."

"In *Through the Looking Glass,*" I said, and then I recited their introduction:

> "The Walrus and the Carpenter
> Were walking close at hand:
> They wept like anything to see
> Such quantities of sand . . ."

Mandie shrugged. "Well, you'll just have to excuse my ignorance and concentrate on my charm," she said.

"I don't know how to break this to you all," said Irene, "but the little one *does* have a handkerchief."

We stared at them. The little one did indeed have a handkerchief, a huge handkerchief, and he was using it to dab at his eyes.

"Is the little one supposed to be the Carpenter?" asked Mandie.

"Yes," I said.

"Then it's all right," she said, "because he's the one that's carrying the saw."

"He is, so help me, God," said Carl. "And, to make the whole thing perfect, he's even wearing an apron."

"So the Carpenter in the poem has to wear an apron, right?" asked Mandie.

"Carroll doesn't say whether he does or not," I said, "but the illustrations by Tenniel show him wearing one. It also shows him with the same square jaw and the same big nose this guy's got."

"They're goddamn doubles," said Carl. "The only thing wrong is that the Walrus isn't a walrus, he just looks like one."

"You watch," said Mandie. "Any minute now he's going to sprout fur all over and grow long fangs."

Then, for the first time, the approaching pair noticed

us. It seemed to give them quite a start. They stood and gaped at us and the little one furtively stuffed his handkerchief out of sight.

"We can't be as surprising as all that!" whispered Irene.

The big one began moving forward, then, in a hesitant, tentative kind of shuffle. The little one edged ahead, too, but he was careful to keep the bulk of his companion between himself and us.

"First contact with the aliens," said Mandie, and Irene and Horace giggled nervously. I didn't respond. I had come to the decision that I was going to quit working for Carl, that I didn't like any of these people about me, except, maybe, Irene, and that these two strangers gave me the honest creeps.

Then the big one smiled, and everything was changed.

I've worked in the entertainment field, in advertising, and in public relations. This means I have come in contact with some of the prime charm boys and girls in our proud land. I have become, therefore, not only a connoisseur of smiles, I am a being equipped with numerous automatic safeguards against them. When a talcumed smoothie comes at me with his brilliant ivories exposed, it only shows he's got something he can bite me with, that's all.

But the smile of the Walrus was something else.

The smile of the Walrus did what a smile hasn't done for me in years—it melted my heart. I use the corn-ball phrase very much on purpose. When I saw his smile, I knew I could trust him; I felt in my marrow that he was gentle and sweet and had nothing but the best intentions. His resemblance to the Walrus in the poem ceased being vaguely chilling and became warmly comical. I loved him as I had loved the teddy bear of my childhood.

"Oh, I *say*," he said, and his voice was an embarrassed boom, "I *do* hope we're not intruding!"

"I daresay we are," squeaked the Carpenter, peeping out from behind his companion.

"The, uhm, fact is," boomed the Walrus, "we didn't even notice you until just back then, you see."

"We were talking, is what," said the Carpenter.

> *They wept like anything to see*
> *Such quantities of sand . . .*

"About sand?" I asked.

The Walrus looked at me with a startled air.

"We *were,* actually, now you come to mention it."

He lifted one huge foot and shook it so that a little trickle of sand spilled out of his shoe.

"The stuff's impossible," he said. "Gets in your clothes, tracks up the carpet."

"Ought to be swept away, it ought," said the Carpenter.

> *'If seven maids with seven mops*
> *Swept it for half a year,*
> *Do you suppose,' the Walrus said,*
> *'That they could get it clear?'*

"It's too much!" said Carl.

"Yes, indeed," said the Walrus, eyeing the sand around him with vague disapproval. "Altogether too much."

Then he turned to us again and we all basked in that smile.

"Permit me to introduce my companion and myself," he said.

"You'll have to excuse George," said the Carpenter, "as he's a bit of a stuffed shirt, don't you know?"

"Be that as it may," said the Walrus, patting the Carpenter on the flat top of his paper hat. "This is Edward Farr, and I am George Tweedy, both at your service. We are, uhm, both a trifle drunk, I'm afraid."

"We are, indeed. We are that."

"As we have just come from a really delightful party, to which we shall soon return."

"Once we've found the fuel, that is," said Farr, waving his saw in the air. By now he had found the courage to come out and face us directly.

"Which brings me to the question," said Tweedy. "Have you seen any *driftwood* lying about the premises? We've been looking high and low and we can't seem to find *any* of the blasted stuff."

"Thought there'd be piles of it," said Farr, "but all there is is sand, don't you see?"

"I would have sworn you were looking for oysters," said Carl.

Again, Tweedy appeared startled.

> *"O oysters come and walk with us!*
> *The Walrus did beseech . . .*

"Oysters?" he asked. "O, no, we've *got* the oysters. All we lack is the means to cook 'em."

"Course we could always use a few more," said Farr, looking at his companion.

"I suppose we *could,* at that," said Tweedy thoughtfully.

"I'm afraid we can't help you fellows with the driftwood problem," said Carl, "but you're more than welcome to a drink."

There was something unfamiliar about the tone of Carl's voice that made my ears perk up. I turned to look at him, and then had difficulty covering up my astonishment.

It was his eyes. For once, for the first time, they were really friendly.

I'm not saying Carl had fishy eyes, blank eyes—not at all. On the surface, that is. On the surface, with his eyes, with his face, with the handling of his entire body, Carl was a master of animation and expression. From sympathetic, heart-felt warmth, all the way to icy rage, and on every stop in-between, Carl was completely convincing.

But only on the surface. Once you got to know Carl,

and it took a while, you realized that none of it was really happening. That was because Carl had died, or been killed, long ago. Possibly in childhood. Possibly he had been born dead. So, under the actor's warmth and rage, the eyes were always the eyes of a corpse.

But now it was different. The friendliness here was genuine, I was sure of it. The smile of Tweedy, of the Walrus, had performed a miracle. Carl had risen from his tomb. I was in honest awe.

"*Delighted,* old chap!" said Tweedy.

They accepted their drinks with obvious pleasure, and we completed the introductions as they sat down to join us. I detected a strong smell of fish when Tweedy sat down beside me but, oddly, I didn't find it offensive in the least. I was glad he'd chosen me to sit by. He turned and smiled at me, and my heart melted a little more.

It soon turned out that the drinking we'd done before had only scratched the surface. Tweedy and Farr were magnificent boozers, and their gusto encouraged us all to follow suit.

We drank absurd toasts and were delighted to discover that Tweedy was an incredible raconteur. His speciality was outrageous fantasy: wild tales involving incongruous objects, events and characters. His invention was endless.

> '*The time has come,*' *the Walrus said,*
> *'To talk of many things:*
> *Of shoes—and ships—and sealing wax—*
> *Of cabbages—and kings—*
> *And why the sea is boiling hot—*
> *And whether pigs have wings.*'

We laughed and drank, and drank and laughed, and I began to wonder why in hell I'd spent my life being such a gloomy, moody sonofabitch, been such a distrustful and suspicious bastard, when the whole secret of everything, the whole core secret, was simply to enjoy it, to take it as it came.

I looked around and grinned, and I didn't care if it was a foolish grin. Everybody looked all right, everybody looked swell, everybody looked better than I'd ever seen them look before.

Irene looked happy, honestly and truly happy. She, too, had found the secret. No more pills for Irene, I thought. Now that she knows the secret, now that she's met Tweedy who's given her the secret, she'll have no more need of those goddamn pills.

And I couldn't believe Horace and Mandie. They had their arms around each other, and their bodies were pressed close together, and they rocked as one being when they laughed at Tweedy's wonderful stories. No more nagging for Mandie, I thought, and no more cringing for Horace, now they've learned the secret.

And then I looked at Carl, laughing and relaxed, and absolutely free of care, absolutely unchilled, finally, at last, after years of—

And then I looked at Carl again.

And then I looked down at my drink, and then I looked at my knees, and then I looked out at the sea, sparkling, clean, remote and impersonal.

And then I realized it had grown cold, quite cold, and that there wasn't a bird or a cloud in the sky.

> *The sea was wet as wet could be,*
> *The sands were dry as dry.*
> *You could not see a cloud, because*
> *No cloud was in the sky:*
> *No birds were flying overhead—*
> *There were no birds to fly.*

That part of the poem was, after all, a perfect description of lifeless earth. It sounded beautiful at first, it sounded benign. But then you read it again and you realized that Carroll was describing barrenness and desolation.

Suddenly Carl's voice broke through and I heard him say:

"Hey, that's a hell of an idea, Tweedy! By God, we'd love to! Wouldn't we, gang?"

The others broke out in an affirmative chorus and they all started scrambling to their feet around me. I looked up at them, like someone who's been awakened from sleep in a strange place, and they grinned down at me like loons.

"Come on, Phil!" cried Irene.

Her eyes were bright and shining, but it wasn't with happiness. I could see that now.

> *'It seems a shame,' the Walrus said,*
> *To play them such a trick . . .'*

I blinked my eyes and stared at them, one after the other.

"Old Phil's had a little too much to drink!" cried Mandie, laughing. "Come on, old Phil! Come on and join the party!"

"What party?" I asked.

I couldn't seem to get located. Everything seemed disoriented and grotesque.

"For Christ's sake, Phil," said Carl, "Tweedy and Farr, here, have invited us to join their party. There're no more drinks left, and they've got plenty!"

I set my plastic cup down carefully on the sand. If they would just shut up for a moment, I thought, I might be able to get the fuzz out of my head.

"Come *along,* sir!" boomed Tweedy jovially. "It's only a pleasant walk!"

> *'O oysters come and walk with us,'*
> *The walrus did beseech.*
> *'A pleasant walk, a pleasant talk,*
> *Along the briny beach . . .'*

He was smiling at me, but the smile didn't work anymore.

"You cannot do with more than four," I told him.

"*Uhm*? What's that?"

> '. . . *we cannot do with more than four,*
> *And give a hand to each.*'

"I said, 'You cannot do with more than four.' "

"He's right, you know," said Farr, the Carpenter.

"Well, uhm, then," said the Walrus, "if you feel you really *can't* come, old chap . . ."

"What, in Christ's name, are you all talking about?" asked Mandie.

"He's hung up on that goddamn poem," said Carl. "Lewis Carroll's got the yellow bastard scared."

"Don't be such a party pooper, Phil!" said Mandie.

"To hell with him," said Carl. And he started off, and all the others followed him. Except Irene.

"Are you sure you really don't want to come, Phil?" she asked.

She looked frail and thin against the sunlight. I realized there really wasn't much of her, and that what there was had taken a terrible beating.

"No," I said. "I don't. Are you sure you want to go?"

"Of course I do, Phil."

I thought of the pills.

"I suppose you do," I said. "I suppose there's really no stopping you."

"No, Phil, there isn't."

And then she stooped and kissed me. Kissed me very gently, and I could feel the dry, chapped surface of her lips and the faint warmth of her breath.

I stood.

"I wish you'd stay," I said.

"I can't," she said.

And then she turned and ran after the others.

I watched them growing smaller and smaller on the beach, following the Walrus and the Carpenter. I watched them come to where the beach curved around the bluff, and watched them disappear behind the bluff.

I looked up at the sky. Pure blue. Impersonal.

"What do you think of this?" I asked it.

Nothing. It hadn't even noticed.

> *'Now, if you're ready, oysters dear,*
> *We can begin to feed.'*
> *'But not on us!' the oysters cried,*
> *Turning a little blue,*
> *'After such kindness, that would be*
> *A dismal thing to do!'*

A dismal thing to do.

I began to run up the beach, toward the bluff. I stumbled now and then because I had had too much to drink. Far too much to drink. I heard small shells crack under my shoes, and the sand made whipping noises.

I fell, heavily, and lay there gasping on the beach. My heart pounded in my chest. I was too old for this sort of footwork. I hadn't had any real exercise in years. I smoked too much and I drank too much. I did all the wrong things. I didn't do any of the right things.

I pushed myself up a little and then I let myself down again. My heart was pounding hard enough to frighten me. I could feel it in my chest, frantically pumping, squeezing blood in and spurting blood out.

Like an oyster pulsing in the sea.

> *'Shall we be trotting home again?'*

My heart was like an oyster.

I got up, fell up, and began to run again, weaving widely, my mouth open and the air burning my throat. I was coated with sweat, streaming with it, and it felt icy in the cold wind.

> *'Shall we be trotting home again?'*

I rounded the bluff, and then I stopped and stood swaying, and then I dropped to my knees.

The pure blue of the sky was unmarked by a single bird or cloud, and nothing stirred on the whole vast stretch of the beach.

> *But answer there came none—*
> *And this was scarcely odd, because . . .*

Nothing stirred, but they were there. Irene and Mandie and Carl and Horace were there, and four others, too. Just around the bluff.

> *'We cannot do with more than four . . .'*

But the Walrus and the Carpenter had taken two trips.

I began to crawl toward them on my knees. My heart, my oyster heart, was pounding too hard to allow me to stand.

The other four had had a picnic, too, very like our own. They, too, had plastic cups and plates, and they, too, had brought bottles. They had sat and waited for the return of the Walrus and the Carpenter.

Irene was right in front of me. Her eyes were open and stared at, but did not see, the sky. The pure blue uncluttered sky. There were a few grains of sand in her left eye. Her face was almost clear of blood. There were only a few flecks of it on her lower chin. The spray from the huge wound in her chest seemed to have traveled mainly downward and to the right. I stretched out my arm and touched her hand.

"Irene," I said.

> *But answer there came none—*
> *And this was scarcely odd, because*
> *They'd eaten every one.*

I looked up at the others. Like Irene, they were, all of them, dead. The Walrus and the Carpenter had eaten the oysters and left the shells.

The Carpenter never had found any firewood, and so they'd eaten them raw. You can eat oysters raw if you want to.

I said her name once more, just for the record, and then I stood and turned from them and walked to the bluff. I rounded the bluff and the beach stretched before me, vast, smooth, empty and remote.

Even as I ran upon it, away from them, it was remote.

Luella Miller

Mary E. Wilkins Freeman

*A lovely demonstration of the affinity,
if not even the identity, of horror with
humor, this is, at the same time, one
of the funniest and most chilling vampire
stories I've ever come across.*

LOSE TO the village street stood the one-story house in which Luella Miller, who had an evil name in the village, had dwelt. She had been dead for years, yet there were those in the village who, in spite of the clearer light which comes on a vantage-point from a long-past danger, half believed in the tale which they had heard from their childhood. In their hearts, although they scarcely would have owned it, was a survival of the wild horror and frenzied fear of their ancestors who had dwelt in the same age with Luella Miller. Young people even would stare with a shudder at the old house as they passed, and children never played around it as was their wont around an untenanted building. Not a window in the old Miller house was broken: the panes reflected the morning sunlight in patches of emerald and blue, and the latch of the sagging front door was never lifted, although no bolt secured it. Since Luella Miller had been carried out of it, the house had had no tenant except one friendless old soul who had no choice between that and the far-off shelter of the open sky. This old woman, who had survived her kindred and friends, lived in the house one week, then one morning no smoke came out of the chimney, and a body of neighbors, a score strong, entered and found her dead in her bed. There were dark whispers as to the cause of her death, and there were those who testified to an expression of fear so exalted that it showed forth the state of the departing soul upon the dead face. The old woman had been hale and hearty when she entered the house, and in seven days she was dead; it seemed that she had fallen a victim to some uncanny power. The minister talked in the pulpit with covert severity against the sin of superstition; still the belief prevailed. Not a soul in the village but would have chosen the almshouse rather than that dwelling. No vagrant, if he heard the tale, would seek shelter beneath that old roof, unhallowed by nearly half a century of superstitious fear.

There was only one person in the village who had actually known Luella Miller. That person was a woman well over eighty, but a marvel of vitality and unextinct youth. Straight as an arrow, with the spring of one recently let loose from the bow of life, she moved about the streets, and she always went to church, rain or shine. She had never married, and had lived alone for years in a house across the road from Luella Miller's.

This woman had none of the garrulousness of age, but never in all her life had she ever held her tongue for any will save her own, and she never spared the truth when she essayed to present it. She it was who bore testimony to the life, evil, though possibly wittingly or designedly so, of Luella Miller, and to her personal appearance. When this old woman spoke—and she had the gift of description, although her thoughts were clothed in the rude vernacular of her native village—one could seem to see Luella Miller as she had really looked. According to this woman, Lydia Anderson by name, Luella Miller had been a beauty of a type rather unusual in New England. She had been a slight, pliant sort of creature, as ready with a strong yielding to fate and as unbreakable as a willow.

She had glimmering lengths of straight, fair hair, which she wore softly looped round a long, lovely face. She had blue eyes full of soft pleading, little slender, clinging hands, and a wonderful grace of motion and attitude.

"Luella Miller used to sit in a way nobody else could if they sat up and studied a week of Sundays," said Lydia Anderson, "and it was a sight to see her walk. If one of them willows over there on the edge of the brook could start up and get its roots free of the ground, and move off, it would go just the way Luella Miller used to. She had a green shot silk she used to wear, too, and a hat with green ribbon streamers, and a lace veil blowing across her face and out sideways, and a green ribbon flyin' from her waist. That was what she come out bride in when she married Erastus Miller. Her name before she was married was Hill. There was always a sight of "I's" in her name, married or single. Erastus Miller was good lookin', too, better lookin' than Luella. Sometimes I used to think that Luella wa'n't so handsome after all. Erastus just about worshiped her. I used to know him pretty well. He lived next door to me, and we went to school together. Folks used to say he was waitin' on me, but he wa'n't. I never thought he was except once or twice when he said things that some girls might have suspected meant somethin'. That was before Luella came here to teach the district school. It was funny how she came to get it, for folks said she hadn't any education, and that one of the big girls, Lottie Henderson, used to do all the teachin' for her, while she sat back and did embroidery work on a cambric pocket-handkerchief. Lottie Henderson was a real smart girl, a splendid scholar, and she just set her eyes by Luella, as all the girls did. Lottie would have made a real smart woman, but she died when Luella had been here about a year—just faded away and died: nobody knew what ailed her. She dragged herself to that schoolhouse and helped Luella teach till the very last minute. The committee all knew how Luella didn't do much of the work herself, but they winked at it. It wa'n't long after

Lottie died that Erastus married her. I always thought he hurried it up because she wa'n't fit to teach. One of the big boys used to help her after Lottie died, but he hadn't much government, and the school didn't do very well, and Luella might have had to give it up, for the committee couldn't have shut their eyes to things much longer. The boy that helped her was a real honest, innocent sort of fellow, and he was a good scholar, too. Folks said he overstudied, and that was the reason he was took crazy the year after Luella married, but I don't know. And I don't know what made Erastus Miller go into consumption of the blood the year after he was married: consumption wa'n't in his family. He just grew weaker and weaker and went almost bent double when he tried to wait on Luella, and he spoke feeble, like an old man. He worked terrible hard till the last trying to save up a little to leave Luella. I've seen him out in the worst storms on a woodsled—he used to cut and sell wood—and he was hunched up on top lookin' more dead than alive. Once I couldn't stand it: I went over and helped him pitch some wood on the cart—I was always strong in my arms. I wouldn't stop for all he told me to, and I guess he was glad enough for the help. That was only a week before he died. He fell on the kitchen floor while he was gettin' breakfast and let Luella lay abed. He did all the sweepin' and the washin' and the ironin' and most of the cookin'. He couldn't bear to have Luella lift her finger, and she let him do for her. She lived like a queen for all the work she did. She didn't even do her sewin'. She said it made her shoulder ache to sew, and poor Erastus's sister Lily used to do all her sewin'. She wa'n't able to, either; she was never strong in her back, but she did it beautifully. She had to, to suit Luella, she was so dreadful particular, I never saw anythin' like the fagottin' and hemstitchin' that Lily Miller did for Luella. She made all Luella's weddin' outfit, and that green silk dress, after Maria Babbit cut it. Maria she cut it for nothin', and she did a lot more cuttin' and fittin' for nothin' for Luella, too. Lily Miller went to live with

Luella after Erastus died. She gave up her home, though she was real attached to it and wa'n't a mite afraid to stay alone. She rented it and she went to live with Luella right away after the funeral."

Then this old woman, Lydia Anderson, who remembered Luella Miller, would go on to relate the story of Lily Miller. It seemed that on the removal of Lily Miller to the house of her dead brother, to live with his widow, the village people first began to talk. This Lily Miller had been hardly past her first youth, and a most robust and blooming woman, rosy-cheeked, with curls of strong, black hair overshadowing round, candid temples and bright dark eyes. It was not six months after she had taken up her residence with her sister-in-law that her rose color faded and her pretty curves became wan hollows. White shadows began to show in the black rings of her hair, and the light died out of her eyes, her features sharpened, and there were pathetic lines at her mouth, which yet wore always an expression of utter sweetness and even happiness. She was devoted to her sister; there was no doubt that she loved her with her whole heart, and was perfectly content in her service. It was her sole anxiety lest she should die and leave her alone.

"The way Lily Miller used to talk about Luella was enough to make you mad and enough to make you cry," said Lydia Anderson. "I've been in there sometimes toward the last when she was too feeble to cook and carried her some blanc-mange or custard—somethin' I thought she might relish, and she'd thank me, and when I asked her how she was, say she felt better than she did yesterday, and asked me if I didn't think she looked better, dreadful pitiful, and say poor Luella had an awful time takin' care of her and doin' the work—she wa'n't strong enough to do anythin'—when all the time Luella wa'n't liftin' her finger and poor Lily didn't get any care except what the neighbors gave her, and Luella eat up everythin' that was carried in for Lily. I had it real straight that she did. Luella used to just sit and cry and do nothin'. She did act real fond of Lily, and she pined away considerable, too. There was those that thought she'd go into a decline herself. But after Lily died, her Aunt Abby Mixter came, and then Luella picked up and grew as fat and rosy as ever. But poor Aunt Abby begun to droop just the way Lily had, and I guess somebody wrote to her married daughter, Mrs. Sam Abbot, who lived in Barre, for she wrote her mother that she must leave right away and come and make her a visit, but Aunt Abby wouldn't go. I can see her now. She was a real good-lookin' woman, tall and large, with a big, square face and a high forehead that looked of itself kind of benevolent and good. She just tended out on Luella as if she had been a baby, and when her married daughter sent for her she wouldn't stir one inch. She'd always thought a lot of her daughter too, but she said Luella needed her and her married daughter didn't. Her daughter kept writin' and writin', but it didn't do any good. Finally she came, and when she saw how bad her mother looked, she broke down and cried and all but went on her knees to have her come away. She spoke her mind out to Luella, too. She told her that she'd killed her husband and everybody that had anythin' to do with her, and she'd thank her to leave her mother alone. Luella went into hysterics, and Aunt Abby was so frightened that she called me after her daughter went. Mrs. Sam Abbot she went away fairly cryin' out loud in the buggy, the neighbors heard her, and well she might, for she never saw her mother again alive. I went in that night when Aunt Abby called for me, standin' in the door with her little green-checked shawl over her head. I can see her now. 'Do come over here, Miss Anderson,' she sung out, kind of gasping for breath. I didn't stop for anythin'. I put over as fast as I could, and when I got there, there was Luella laughin' and cryin' all together, and Aunt Abby trying to hush her, and all the time she herself was white as a sheet and shakin' so she could hardly stand. 'For the land sakes, Mrs. Mixter,' says I, 'you look worse than she does. You ain't fit to be up out of your bed.'

" 'Oh, there ain't anythin' the matter with me,' says she. Then she went on talkin' to Luella. 'There, there, don't, don't, poor little lamb,' says she. 'Aunt Abby is here. She ain't goin' away and leave you. Don't, poor little lamb.'

" 'Do leave her with me, Mrs. Mixter, and you get back to bed,' says I, for Aunt Abby had been layin' down considerable lately, though somehow she contrived to do the work.

" 'I'm well enough,' says she. 'Don't you think she had better have the doctor, Miss Anderson?'

" 'The doctor,' says I, 'I think *you* had better have the doctor. I think you need him much worse than some folks I could mention.' And I looked right straight at Luella Miller laughin' and cryin' and goin' on as if she was the center of all creation. All the time she was actin' so— seemed as if she was too sick to sense anythin'—she was keepin' a sharp lookout as to how we took it out of the corner of one eye. I see her. You could never cheat me about Luella Miller. Finally I got real mad and I run home and I got a bottle of valerian I had, and I poured some boilin' hot water on a handful of catnip, and I mixed up that catnip tea with most half a wineglass of valerian, and I went with it over to Luella's. I marched right up to Luella, a-holdin' out of that cup, all smokin'. 'Now,' says I, 'Luella Miller, *you swaller this!*'

" 'What is—what is it, oh, what is it?' she sort of screeches out. Then she goes off a-laughin' enough to kill.

" 'Poor lamb, poor little lamb,' says Aunt Abby, standin' over her, all kind of tottery, and tryin' to bathe her head with camphor.

" '*You swaller this right down,*' says I. And I didn't waste any ceremony. I just took hold of Luella Miller's chin and I tipped her head back, and I caught her mouth open with laughin', and I clapped that cup to her lips, and I fairly hollered at her: 'Swaller, swaller, swaller!' and she gulped it right down. She had to, and I guess it did her good. Anyhow, she stopped cryin' and laughin' and let me put her to bed, and she went to sleep like a baby inside of half an hour. That was more than poor Aunt Abby did. She lay awake all that night and I stayed with her, though she tried not to have me; said she wa'n't sick enough for watchers. But I stayed, and I made some good cornmeal gruel and I fed her a teaspoon every little while all night long. It seemed to me as if she was jest dyin' from bein' all wore out. In the mornin' as soon as it was light I run over to the Bisbees and sent Johnny Bisbee for the doctor. I told him to tell the doctor to hurry, and he come pretty quick. Poor Aunt Abby didn't seem to know much of anythin' when he got there. You couldn't hardly tell she breathed, she was so used up. When the doctor had gone, Luella came into the room lookin' like a baby in her ruffled nightgown. I can see her now. Her eyes were as blue and her face all pink and white like a blossom, and she looked at Aunt Abby in the bed sort of innocent and surprised. 'Why,' says she, 'Aunt Abby ain't got up yet?'

" 'No, she ain't,' says I, pretty short.

" 'I thought I didn't smell the coffee,' says Luella.

" 'Coffee,' says I. 'I guess if you have coffee this mornin' you'll make it yourself.'

" 'I never made the coffee in all my life,' says she, dreadful astonished. 'Erastus always made the coffee as long as he lived, and then Lily she made it, and then Aunt Abby made it. I don't believe I *can* make the coffee, Miss Anderson.'

" 'You can make it or go without, jest as you please,' says I.

" 'Aint Aunt Abby goin' to get up?' says she.

" 'I guess she won't get up,' says I, 'sick as she is.' I was gettin' madder and madder. There was somethin' about that little pink-and-white thing standin' there and talkin' about coffee, when she had killed so many better folks than she was, and had jest killed another, that made me feel 'most as if I wished somebody would up and kill her before she had a chance to do any more harm.

" 'Is Aunt Abby sick?' says Luella, as if she was sort of aggrieved and injured.

" 'Yes,' says I, 'she's sick, and she's goin' to die, and then you'll be left alone, and you'll have to do for yourself and wait on yourself, or do without things.' I don't know but I was sort of hard, but it was the truth, and if I was any harder than Luella Miller had been I'll give up. I ain't never been sorry that I said it. Well, Luella, she up and had hysterics again at that, and I jest let her have 'em. All I did was to bundle her into the room on the other side of the entry where Aunt Abby couldn't hear her, if she wa'n't past it—I don't know but she was—and set her down hard in a chair and told her not to come back into the other room, and she minded. She had her hysterics in there till she got tired. When she found out that nobody was comin' to coddle her and do for her she stopped. At least I suppose she did. I had all I could do with poor Aunt Abby tryin' to keep the breath of life in her. The doctor had told me that she was dreadful low, and give me some very strong medicine to give to her in drops real often, and told me real particular about the nourishment. Well, I did as he told me real faithful till she wa'n't able to swaller any longer. Then I had her daughter sent for. I had begun to realize that she wouldn't last any time at all. I hadn't realized it before, though I spoke to Luella the way I did. The doctor he came, and Mrs. Sam Abbot, but when she got there it was too late; her mother was dead. Aunt Abby's daughter just give one look at her mother layin' there, then she turned sort of sharp and sudden and looked at me.

" 'Where is she?' says she, and I knew she meant Luella.

" 'She's out in the kitchen,' says I. 'She's too nervous to see folks die. She's afraid it will make her sick.'

"The Doctor he speaks up then. He was a young man. Old Doctor Park had died the year before, and this was a young fellow just out of college. 'Mrs. Miller is not strong,' says he, kind of severe, 'and she is quite right in not agitating herself.'

" 'You are another, young man; she's got her pretty claw on you,' thinks I, but I didn't say anythin' to him. I just said over to Mrs. Sam Abbot that Luella was in the kitchen, and Mrs. Sam Abbot she went out there, and I went, too, and I never heard anythin' like the way she talked to Luella Miller. I felt pretty hard to Luella myself, but this was more than I ever would have dared to say. Luella she was too scared to go into hysterics. She jest flopped. She seemed to jest shrink away to nothin' in that kitchen chair, with Mrs. Sam Abbot standin' over her and talkin' and tellin' her the truth. I guess the truth was most too much for her and no mistake, because Luella presently actually did faint away, and there wa'n't any sham about it, the way I always suspected there was about them hysterics. She fainted dead away and we had to lay her flat on the floor, and the Doctor he came runnin' out and he said somethin' about a weak heart dreadful fierce to Mrs. Sam Abbot, but she wa'n't a mite scared. She faced him jest as white as even Luella was layin' there lookin' like death and the Doctor feelin' of her pulse.

" 'Weak heart,' says she, 'weak heart; weak fiddlesticks! There ain't nothin' weak about that woman. She's got strength enough to hang onto other folks till she kills 'em. Weak? It was my poor mother that was weak: this woman killed her as sure as if she had taken a knife to her.'

"But the Doctor he didn't pay much attention. He was bendin' over Luella layin' there with her yellow hair all streamin' and her pretty pink-and-white face all pale, and her blue eyes like stars gone out, and he was holdin' onto her hand and smoothin' her forehead, and tellin' me to get the brandy in Aunt Abby's room, and I was sure as I wanted to be that Luella had got somebody else to hang onto, now Aunt Abby was gone, and I thought of poor

Erastus Miller, and I sort of pitied the poor young Doctor, led away by a pretty face, and I made up my mind I'd see what I could do.

"I waited till Aunt Abby had been dead and buried about a month, and the Doctor was goin' to see Luella steady and folks were beginnin' to talk; then one evenin', when I knew the Doctor had been called out of town and wouldn't be round, I went over to Luella's. I found her all dressed up in a blue muslin with white polka dots on it, and her hair curled jest as pretty, and there wa'n't a young girl in the place could compare with her. There was somethin' about Luella Miller seemed to draw the heart right out of you, but she didn't draw it out of *me*. She was settin' rocking in the chair by her sittin-room window, and Maria Brown had gone home. Maria Brown had been in to help her, or rather to do the work, for Luella wa'n't helped when she didn't do anythin'. Maria Brown was real capable and she didn't have any ties; she wa'n't married, and lived alone, so she'd offered. I couldn't see why she should do the work any more than Luella; she wa'n't any too strong; but she seemed to think she could and Luella seemed to think so, too, so she went over and did all the work—washed, and ironed, and baked, while Luella sat and rocked. Maria didn't live long afterward. She began to fade away just the same fashion the others had. Well, she was warned, but she acted real mad when folks said anythin': said Luella was a poor, abused woman, too delicate to help herself, and they'd ought to be ashamed, and if she died helpin' them that couldn't help themselves she would—and she did.

" 'I s'pose Maria has gone home,' says I to Luella, when I had gone in and sat down opposite her.

" 'Yes, Maria went half an hour ago, after she had got supper and washed the dishes,' says Luella, in her pretty way.

" 'I suppose she had got a lot of work to do in her own house tonight,' says I, kind of bitter, but that was all thrown away on Luella Miller. It seemed to her right that other folks that wa'n't any better able than she was herself should wait on her, and she couldn't get it through her head that anybody should think it *wa'n't* right.

" 'Yes,' says Luella, real sweet and pretty, 'yes, she said she had to do her washin' tonight. She has let it go for a fortnight along of comin' over here.'

" 'Why don't she stay home and do her washin' instead of comin' over here and doin' *your* work, when you are just as well able, and enough sight more so, than she is to do it?' says I.

"Then Luella she looked at me like a baby who has a rattle shook at it. She sort of laughed as innocent as you please. 'Oh, I can't do the work myself, Miss Anderson,' says she. 'I never did. Maria *has* to do it.'

"Then I spoke out: 'Has to do it!' says I. 'Has to do it!' She don't have to do it, either. Maria Brown has her own home and enough to live on. She ain't beholden to you to come over here and slave for you and kill herself.'

"Luella she jest set and stared at me for all the world like a doll-baby that was so abused that it was comin' to life.

" 'Yes,' says I, 'she's killin' herself. She's goin' to die just the way Erastus did, and Lily, and your Aunt Abby. You're killin' her jest as you did them. I don't know what there is about you, but you seem to bring a curse,' says I. 'You kill everybody that is fool enough to care anythin' about you and do for you.'

"She stared at me and she was pretty pale.

" 'And Maria ain't the only one you're goin' to kill,' says I. 'You're goin' to kill Doctor Malcom before you're done with him.'

"Then a red color came flamin' all over her face. 'I ain't goin' to kill him, either,' says she, and she begun to cry.

"Yes, you *be*!' says I. Then I spoke as I had never spoke before. You see, I felt it on account of Erastus. I told her that she hadn't any business to think of another man after she'd been married to one that had died for

her: that she was a dreadful woman; and she was, that's
true enough, but sometimes I have wondered lately if she
knew it—if she wa'n't like a baby with scissors in its hand
cuttin' everybody without knowin' what it was doin'.

Luella she kept gettin' paler and paler, and she never
took her eyes off my face. There was somethin' awful
about the way she looked at me and never spoke one
word. After awhile I quit talkin' and I went home. I
watched that night, but her lamp went out before nine
o'clock, and when Doctor Malcom came drivin' past and
sort of slowed up he see there wa'n't any light and he
drove along. I saw her sort of shy out of meetin' the next
Sunday, too, so he shouldn't go home with her, and I begun to think mebbe she did have some conscience after
all. It was only a week after that that Maria Brown
died—sort of sudden at the last, though everybody had
seen it was comin'. Well, then there was a good deal of
feelin' and pretty dark whispers. Folks said the days of
witchcraft had come again, and they were pretty shy of
Luella. She acted sort of offish to the Doctor and he
didn't go there, and there wa'n't anybody to do anythin'
for her. I don't know how she *did* get along. I wouldn't go
in there and offer to help her—not because I was afraid
of dyin' like the rest, but I thought she was just as well
able to do her own work as I was to do it for her, and I
thought it was about time that she did it and stopped killin' other folks. But it wa'n't very long before folks began
to say that Luella herself was goin' into a decline jest the
way her husband, and Lily, and Aunt Abby and the others had, and I saw myself that she looked pretty bad. I
used to see her goin' past from the store with a bundle as
if she could hardly crawl, but I remembered how Erastus
used to wait and 'tend when he couldn't hardly put one
foot before the other, and I didn't go out to help her.

"But at last one afternoon I saw the Doctor come
drivin' up like mad with his medicine chest, and Mrs.
Babbit came in after supper and said that Luella was real
sick.

" 'I'd offer to go in and nurse her,' says she, 'but I've got my children to consider, and mebbe it ain't true what they say, but it's queer how many folks that have done for her have died.'

"I didn't say anythin', but I considered how she had been Erastus's wife and how he had set his eyes by her, and I made up my mind to go in the next mornin', unless she was better, and see what I could do; but the next mornin' I see her at the window, and pretty soon she came steppin' out as spry as you please, and a little while afterward Mrs. Babbit came in and told me that the Doctor had got a girl from out of town, a Sarah Jones, to come there, and she said she was pretty sure that the Doctor was goin' to marry Luella.

"I saw him kiss her in the door that night myself, and I knew it was true. The woman came that afternoon, and the way she flew around was a caution. I don't believe Luella had swept since Maria died. She swept and dusted, and washed and ironed; wet clothes and dusters and carpets were flyin' over there all day, and every time Luella set her foot out when the Doctor wa'n't there there was that Sarah Jones helpin' of her up and down the steps, as if she hadn't learned to walk.

"Well, everybody knew that Luella and the Doctor were goin' to be married, but it wa'n't long before they began to talk about his lookin' so poorly, jest as they had about the others; and they talked about Sarah Jones, too.

"Well, the Doctor did die, and he wanted to be married first, so as to leave what little he had to Luella, but he died before the minister could get there, and Sarah Jones died a week afterward.

"Well, that wound up everything for Luella Miller. Not another soul in the whole town would lift a finger for her. There got to be a sort of panic. Then she began to droop in good earnest. She used to have to go to the store herself, for Mrs. Babbit was afraid to let Tommy go for her, and I've seen her goin' past and stoppin' every two or three steps to rest. Well, I stood it as long as I could, but one day I see her comin' with her arms full and stoppin' to lean against the Babbit fence, and I run out and took her bundles and carried them to her house. Then I went home and never spoke one word to her though she called after me dreadful kind of pitiful. Well, that night I was taken sick with a chill, and I was sick as I wanted to be for two weeks. Mrs. Babbit had seen me run out to help Luella and she came in and told me I was goin' to die on account of it. I didn't know whether I was or not, but I considered I had done right by Erastus's wife.

"That last two weeks Luella she had a dreadful hard time, I guess. She was pretty sick, and as near as I could make out nobody dared go near her. I don't know as she was really needin' anythin' very much, for there was enough to eat in her house and it was warm weather, and she made out to cook a little flour gruel every day, I know, but I guess she had a hard time, she that had been so petted and done for all her life.

"When I got so I could go out, I went over there one morning. Mrs. Babbit had just come in to say she hadn't seen any smoke and she didn't know but it was some-body's duty to go in, but she couldn't help thinkin' of her children, and I got right up, though I hadn't been out of the house for two weeks, and I went in there, and Luella she was layin' on the bed, and she was dyin'.

"She lasted all that day and into the night. But I sat there after the new doctor had gone away. Nobody else dared to go there. It was about midnight that I left her for a minute to run home and get some medicine I had been takin', for I begun to feel rather bad.

"It was a full moon that night, and just as I started out of my door to cross the street back to Luella's, I stopped short, for I saw something."

Lydia Anderson at this juncture always said with a certain defiance that she did not expect to be believed, and then proceeded in a hushed voice:

"I saw what I saw, and I know I saw it, and I will swear on my death bed that I saw it. I saw Luella Miller and Erastus Miller, and Lily, and Aunt Abby, and Maria, and the Doctor, and Sarah, all goin' out of her door, and all but Luella shone white in the moonlight, and they were all helpin' her along till she seemed to fairly fly in the midst of them. Then it all disappeared. I stood a minute with my heart poundin', then I went over there. I thought of goin' for Mrs. Babbit, but I thought she'd be afraid. So I went alone, though I knew what had happened. Luella was layin' real peaceful, dead on her bed."

This was the story that the old woman, Lydia Anderson, told, but the sequel was told by the people who survived her, and this is the tale which had become folklore in the village.

Lydia Anderson died when she was eighty-seven. She had continued wonderfully hale and hearty for one of her years until about two weeks before her death.

One bright moonlight evening she was sitting beside a window in her parlor when she made a sudden exclamation, and was out of the house and across the street before the neighbor who was taking care of her could stop her. She followed as fast as possible and found Lydia Anderson stretched on the ground before the door of Luella Miller's deserted house, and she was quite dead.

The next night there was a red gleam of fire athwart the moonlight and the old house of Luella Miller was burned to the ground. Nothing is now left of it except a few old cellar stones and a lilac bush, and in summer a helpless trail of morning glories among the weeds, which might be considered emblematic of Luella herself.

The Idol With Hands of Clay

Sir Frederick Treves

It really would not be fair if I did not warn you that this story is absolutely horrifying. The most awful thing about it, though, is not what takes place during the tale, but the thought of the hell which would follow after.

HE GOOD SURGEON is born,
not made. He is a complex product in any case, and often
something of a prodigy. His qualities cannot be expressed
by diplomas nor appraised by university degrees. It may
be possible to ascertain what he knows, but no examination can elicit what he can do. He must know the human body as a forester knows his wood; must know it
even better than he, must know the roots and branches of
every tree, the source and wanderings of every rivulet, the
banks of every alley, the flowers of every glade. As a surgeon, moreover, he must be learned in the moods and
troubles of the wood, must know of the wild winds that
may rend it, of the savage things that lurk in its secret
haunts, of the strangling creepers that may throttle its
sturdiest growth, of the rot and mold that may make dust
of its very heart. As an operator, moreover, he must be a
deft handicraftsman and a master of touch.

He may have all these acquirements and yet be found
wanting; just as a man may succeed when shooting at a
target, but fail when faced by a charging lion. He may be
a clever manipulator and yet be mentally clumsy. He may

even be brilliant, but Heaven help the poor soul who has to be operated upon by a brilliant surgeon. Brilliancy is out of place in surgery. It is pleasing in the juggler who plays with knives in the air, but it causes anxiety in an operating theater.

The surgeon's hands must be delicate, but they must also be strong. He needs a lacemaker's fingers and a seaman's grip. He must have courage, be quick to think and prompt to act, be sure of himself and captain of the venture he commands. The surgeon has often to fight for another's life. I conceive of him then not as a massive Hercules wrestling ponderously with Death for the body of Alcestis, but as a nimble man in doublet and hose who, over a prostrate form, fights Death with a rapier.

These reflections were the outcome of an incident which had set me thinking of the equipment of a surgeon and of what is needed to fit him for his work. The episode concerned a young medical man who had started practice in a humble country town. His student career had been meritorious and indeed distinguished. He had obtained an entrance scholarship at his medical school, had collected many laudatory certificates, had been awarded a gold medal and had become a Fellow of the Royal College of Surgeons. His inclination was towards surgery. He considered surgery to be his *métier*. Although circumstances had condemned him to the drab life of a family doctor in a little town, he persisted that he was, first and foremost, a surgeon, and, indeed, on his door-plate had inverted the usual wording and had described himself as "surgeon and physician." In his hospital days he had assisted at many operations, but his opportunities of acting as a principal had been few and insignificant. In a small practice in a small town surgical opportunities are rare. There was in the place a cottage hospital with six beds, but it was mostly occupied by medical cases, by patients with rheumatism or pneumonia, by patients who had to submit to the surgical indignity of being poulticed and of being treated by mere physic. Cases worthy of a Fellow of the Royal College of Surgeons were very few, and even these seldom soared in interest above an abscess or a broken leg.

Just before the young doctor settled down to practice he married. It was a very happy union. The bride was the daughter of a neighboring farmer. She had spent her life in the country, was more familiar with the ways of fowls and ducks than with the ways of the world, while a sunbonnet became her better than a Paris toque. She was as pretty as the milkmaid of a pastoral picture with her pink-and-white complexion, her laughing eyes and her rippled hair.

Her chief charm was her radiant delight in the mere joy of living. The small world in which she moved was to her always in the sun, and the sun was that of summer. There was no town so pretty as her little town, and no house so perfect as "the doctor's" in the High Street. "The doctor's" was a Georgian house with windows of many panes, with a fan-light like a surprised eyebrow over the entry and a self-conscious brass knocker on the door. The house was close to the pavement, from which it was separated by a line of white posts connected by loops of chain. Passers-by could look over the low green wooden blinds into the dining-room and see the table covered with worn magazines, for the room was intended to imitate a Harley Street waiting-room. They could also see the bright things on the sideboard, the wedding-present biscuit box, the gong hanging from two cow-horns and the cup won at some hospital sports. To the young wife there never was such a house, nor such furniture, nor such ornaments, nor, as she went about with a duster from room to room, could there be a greater joy than that of keeping everything polished and bright.

Her most supreme adoration, however, was for her husband. He was so handsome, so devoted, and so amazingly clever. His learning was beyond the common grasp, and the depths of his knowledge unfathomable. When a friend came in at night to smoke a pipe she would sit silent and open-mouthed, lost in admiration of her husband's dazzling intellect. How glibly he would talk of metabolism and blood-pressure; how marvelously he endowed common things with mystic significance when he discoursed upon the value of calories of a pound of steak, or upon the vitamins that enrich the common bean, or even the more common cabbage. It seemed to her that behind the tiny world she knew there was a mysterious universe with which her well-beloved was as familiar as was she with the contents of her larder.

She was supremely happy and content, while her husband bestowed upon her all the affection of which he was capable. He was naturally vain, but her idolatry made him vainer. She considered him wonderful, and he was beginning to think her estimate had some truth in it. She was so proud of him that she rather wearied her friends by the tale of his achievements. She pressed him to allow her to have his diploma and his more florid certificates framed and hung up in the consulting room, but he had said with chilling superiority that such things "were not done," so that she could only console herself by adoring the modesty of men of genius.

One day this happy, ever-busy lady was seized with appendicitis. She had had attacks in her youth, but they had passed away. This attack, although not severe, was graver, and her husband determined, quite wisely, that an operation was necessary. He proposed to ask a well-known surgeon in a neighboring city to undertake this measure. He told his wife, of course, of his intention, but she would have none of it. "No," she said, "she would not be operated on by stuffy old Mr. Heron.* He was no good. She could not bear him even to touch her. If an operation was necessary no one should do it but her husband. He was so clever, such a surgeon, and so up-to-date. Old Heron was a fossil and behind the times. No! Her clever Jimmy should do it and no one else. She could trust no one else. In his wonderful hands she would be

* The name is fictitious.

safe, and would be running about again in the garden in no time. What was the use of a fine surgeon if his own wife was denied his precious help!"

The husband made no attempt to resist her wish. He contemplated the ordeal with dread, but was so influenced by her fervid flattery that he concealed from her the fact that the prospect made him faint of heart and that he had even asked himself: "Can I go through with it?"

He told me afterwards that his miserable vanity decided him. He could not admit that he lacked either courage or competence. He saw, moreover, the prospect of making an impression. The town people would say: "Here is a surgeon so sure of himself that he carries out a grave operation on his own wife without a tremor." Then, again, his assistant would be his fellow-practitioner in the town. How impressed he would be by the operator's skill, by his coolness, by the display of the latest type of instrument, and generally by his very advanced methods. It was true that it was the first major operation he had ever undertaken, but he no longer hesitated. He must not imperil his wife's faith in him nor fail to realize her conception of his powers. As he said to me more than once, it was his vanity that decided him.

He read up the details of the operation in every available manual he possessed. It seemed to be a simple procedure. Undoubtedly in nine cases out of ten it *is* a simple measure. His small experience, as an onlooker, had been limited to the nine cases. He had never met with the tenth. He hardly believed in it. The operation as he had watched it at the hospital seemed so simple, but he forgot that the work of expert hands does generally appear simple.

The elaborate preparations for the operation—made with anxious fussiness and much clinking of steel—were duly completed. The lady was brought into the room appointed for the operation andd placed on the table. She looked very young. Her hair, parted at the back, was arranged in two long plaits, one on either side of her face, as if she were a school-girl. She had insisted on a pink bow at the end of each plait, pleading that they were cheerful. She smiled as she saw her husband standing in the room looking very gaunt and solemn in his operating dress—a garb of linen that made him appear half-monk, half-mechanic. She held her hand towards him, but he said he could not take it as his own hand was sterilized. Her smile vanished for a moment at the rebuke, but came back again as she said: "Now don't look so serious, Jimmy; I am not the least afraid. I know that with you I am safe and that you will make me well, but be sure you are by my side when I awake, for I want to see you as I open my eyes. Wonderful boy!"

The operation was commenced. The young doctor told me that as he cut with his knife into that beautiful white skin and saw the blood well up behind it a lump rose in his throat and he felt that he must give up the venture. His vanity, however, urged him on. His doctor friend was watching him. He must impress him with his coolness and his mastery of the position. He talked of casual things to show that he was quite at ease, but his utterances were artificial and forced.

For a time all went well. He was showing off, he felt, with some effect. But when the depths of the wound were reached a condition of things was found which puzzled him. Structures were confused and matted together, and so obscured as to be unrecognizable. He had read of nothing like this in his books. It was the tenth case. He became uneasy, and indeed, alarmed, as one who had lost his way. He ceased to chatter. He tried to retain his attitude of coolness and command. He must be bold, he kept saying to himself. He made blind efforts to find his course, became wild and finally reckless. Then a terrible thing happened. There was a tear—something gave way—something gushed forth. His heart seemed to stop. He thought he should faint. A cold sweat broke out upon his brow. He ceased to speak. His trembling fingers groped aimlessly in the depths of the wound. His friend asked: "What has happened?" He replied with a sickly fury: "Shut up!"

He tried then to repair the damage he had done; took up instrument after instrument and dropped them again until the patient's body was covered with soiled and discarded forceps, knives and clamps. He wiped the sweat from his brow with his hand and left a wide streak of blood across his forehead. His knees shook and he stamped to try to stop them. He cursed the doctor who was helping him, crying out: "For God's sake do this," or "For God's sake don't do that"; sighed like a suffocating man; looked vacantly round the room as if for help; looked appealingly to his wife's masked face for some sign of her tender comfort, but she was more than dumb. Frenzied with despair, he told the nurse to send for Mr. Heron. It was a hopeless mission, since that surgeon—even if at home—could not arrive for hours.

He tried again and again to close the awful rent, but he was now nearly dropping with terror and exhaustion. Then the anaesthetist said in a whisper: "How much longer will you be? Her pulse is failing. She cannot stand much more." He felt that he must finish or die. He finished in a way. He closed the wound, and then sank on a stool with his face buried in his blood-stained hands, while the nurse and the doctor applied the necessary dressing.

The patient was carried back to her bedroom, but he dared not follow. The doctor who had helped him crept away without speaking a word. He was left alone in this dreadful room with its hideous reminders of what he had done. He wandered about, looked aimlessly out of the window, but saw nothing, picked up his wife's handkerchief which was lying on the table, crunched it in his hand, and then dropped it on the floor as the red horror of it all flooded his brain. What had he done to her? She! She of all women in the world!

He caught a sight of himself in the glass. His face was smeared with blood. He looked inhuman and unrecognizable. It was not himself he saw: it was a murderer with the brand of Cain upon his brow. He looked again at her handkerchief on the ground. It was the last thing her hand had closed upon. It was a piece of her lying amid this scene of unspeakable horror. It was like some ghastly item of evidence in a murder story. He could not touch it. He could not look at it. He covered it with a towel.

In a while he washed his hands and face, put on his coat and walked into the bedroom. The blind was down; the place was almost dark; the atmosphere was laden with the smell of ether. He could see the form of his wife on the bed, but she was so still and seemed so thin. The coverlet appeared so flat, except where the points of her feet raised a little ridge. Her face was as white as marble. Although the room was very silent, he could not hear her breathe. On one side of the bed stood the nurse, and on the other side the anaesthetist. Both were motionless. They said nothing. Indeed, there was nothing to say. They did not even look up when he came in. He touched his wife's hand, but it was cold and he could feel no pulse.

In about two hours Heron, the surgeon, arrived. The young doctor saw him in an adjacent bedroom, gave him an incoherent, spasmodic account of the operation, laid emphasis on unsurmountable difficulties, gabbled something about an accident, tried to excuse himself, maintained that the fault was not his, but that circumstances were against him.

The surgeon's examination of the patient was very brief. He went into the room alone. As he came out he closed the door after him. The husband, numb with terror, was awaiting him in the lobby. The surgeon put his hand on the wretched man's shoulder, shook his head and, without uttering a single word, made his way down the stairs. He nearly stumbled over a couple of shrinking, white-faced maids who had crept up the stairs in the hope of hearing something of their young mistress.

As he passed one said: "Is she better, doctor?" but he merely shook his head, and without a word walked out into the sunny street where some children were dancing to a barrel-organ.

The husband told me that he could not remember what he did during these portentous hours after the operation. He could not stay in the bedroom. He wandered about the house. He went into his consulting room and pulled out some half-dozen works on surgery with the idea of gaining some comfort or guidance; but he never saw a word on the printed page. He went into the dispensary and looked over the rows of bottles on the shelves to see if he could find anything, any drug, any elixir that would help. He crammed all sorts of medicines into his pocket and took them upstairs, but, as he entered the room, he forgot all about them, and when he found them in his coat a week later he wondered how they had got there. He remembered a pallid maid coming up to him and saying: "Lunch is ready, sir." He thought her mad.

He told me that among the horrors that haunted him during these hours of waiting not the least were the flippant and callous thoughts that would force themselves into his mind with fiendish brutality. There was, for example, a scent bottle on his wife's table—a present from her aunt. He found himself wondering why her aunt had given it to her and when, what she had paid for it, and what the aunt would say when she heard her niece was dead. Worse than that, he began composing in his mind an obituary notice for the newspapers. How should he word it? Should he say "Beloved wife," or "dearly loved wife," and should he add all his medical qualifications? It was terrible. Terrible, too, was his constant longing to tell his wife of the trouble he was in and to be comforted by her.

Shortly after the surgeon left, the anaesthetist noticed some momentary gleam of consciousness in the patient. The husband hurried in. The end had come. His wife's face was turned towards the window. The nurse lifted the blind a little so that the light fell full upon her. She opened her eyes and at once recognized her husband. She tried to move her hand towards him, but it fell listless on the sheet. A smile—radiant, grateful, adoring—illumined her face, and as he bent over her he heard her whisper: "Wonderful boy."

My Favorite Murder

Ambrose Bierce

*Ambrose Bierce once headed a chapter with
A Man Though Naked May Be in Rags,
describing a horribly mauled cadaver, and
in his Devil's Dictionary he defined
happiness as "the contemplation of other
people's misery." It takes a fellow
like that to write a story like this.*

AVING murdered my mother under circumstances of singular atrocity, I was arrested and put upon my trial, which lasted seven years. In summing up, the judge of the Court of Acquittal remarked that it was one of the most ghastly crimes that he had ever been called upon to explain away.

At this my counsel rose and said:

"May it please your honor, crimes are ghastly or agreeable only by comparison. If you were familiar with the details of my client's previous murder of his uncle, you would discern in his later offense something in the nature of tender forbearance and filial consideration for the feelings of the victim. The appalling ferocity of the former assassination was indeed inconsistent with any hypothesis but that of guilt; and had it not been for the fact that the honorable judge before whom he was tried was the president of a life insurance company which took risks on hanging, and in which my client held a policy, it is impossible to see how he could have been decently acquitted. If your honor would like to hear about it for the instruction and guidance of your honor's mind, this unfortunate man, my client, will consent to give himself the pain of relating it under oath."

The district attorney said: "Your honor, I object. Such a statement would be in the nature of evidence, and the testimony in this case is closed. The prisoner's statement should have been introduced three years ago, in the spring of 1881."

"In a statutory sense," said the judge, "you are right, and in the Court of Objections and Technicalities you would get a ruling in your favor. But not in a Court of Acquittal. The objection is overruled."

"I except," said the district attorney.

"You cannot do that," the judge said. "I must remind you that in order to take an exception you must first get this case transferred for a time to the Court of Exceptions upon a formal motion duly supported by affidavits. A motion to that effect by your predecessor in office was denied by me during the first year of this trial.

"Mr. Clerk, swear the prisoner."

The customary oath having been administered, I made the following statement, which impressed the judge with so strong a sense of the comparative triviality of the offense for which I was on trial that he made no further search for mitigating circumstances, but simply instructed the jury to acquit, and I left the court without a stain upon my reputation:

"I was born in 1856 in Kalamakee, Mich., of honest and reputable parents, one of whom Heaven has mercifully spared to comfort me in my later years. In 1867 the family came to California and settled near Nigger Head, where my father opened a road agency and prospered beyond the dreams of avarice. He was a silent, saturnine man then, though his increasing years have now somewhat relaxed the austerity of his disposition, and I believe that nothing but his memory of the sad event for which I

am now on trial prevents him from manifesting a genuine
hilarity.

"Four years after we had set up the road agency an
itinerant preacher came along, and having no other way
to pay for the night's lodging which we gave him, favored
us with an exhoration of such power that, praise God, we
were all converted to religion. My father at once sent for
his brother, the Hon. William Ridley of Stockton, and on
his arrival turned over the agency to him, charging him
nothing for the franchise or plant—the latter consisting of
a Winchester rifle, a sawnoff shotgun, and an assortment
of masks made out of flour sacks. The family then moved
to Ghost Rock and opened a dance house. It was called
'The Saints' Rest Hurdy-Gurdy,' and the proceedings each
night began with prayer. It was there that my now sainted
mother, by her grace in the dance, acquired the *so-
briquet* of 'The Bucking Walrus.'

"In the fall of '75 I had occasion to visit Coyote, on
the road to Mahala, and took the stage at Ghost Rock.
There were four other passengers. About three miles beyond Nigger Head, persons whom I identified as my
Uncle William and his two sons held up the stage. Finding
nothing in the express box, they went through the passengers. I acted a most honorable part in the affair, placing
myself in line with the others, holding up my hands and
permitting myself to be deprived of forty dollars and a
gold watch. From my behavior no one could have suspected that I knew the gentlemen who gave the entertainment. A few days later, when I went to Nigger Head and
asked for the return of my money and watch, my uncle
and cousins swore they knew nothing of the matter, and
they affected a belief that my father and I had done the
job ourselves in dishonest violation of commercial good
faith. Uncle William even threatened to retaliate by starting an opposition dance house at Ghost Rock. As 'The
Saints' Rest' had become rather unpopular, I saw that this
would assuredly ruin it and prove a paying enterprise, so I
told my uncle that I was willing to overlook the past if he

would take me into the scheme and keep the partnership a secret from my father. This fair offer he rejected, and then I perceived that it would be better and more satisfactory if he were dead.

"My plans to that end were soon perfected, and communicating them to my dear parents, I had the gratification of receiving their approval. My father said he was proud of me, and my mother promised that, although her religion forbade her to assist in taking human life, I should have the advantage of her prayers for my success. As a preliminary measure, looking to my security in case of detection, I made an application for membership in that powerful order, the Knights of Murder, and in due course was received as a member of the Ghost Rock Commandery. On the day that my probation ended I was for the first time permitted to inspect the records of the order and learn who belonged to it—all the rites of initiation having been conducted in masks. Fancy my delight when, in looking over the roll of membership, I found the third name to be that of my uncle, who indeed was junior vice-chancellor of the order! Here was an opportunity exceeding my wildest dreams—to murder I could add insubordination and treachery. It was what my good mother would have called 'a special Providence.'

"At about this time something occurred which caused my cup of joy, already full, to overflow on all sides, a circular cataract of bliss. Three men, strangers in that locality, were arrested for the stage robbery in which I had lost my money and watch. They were brought to trial and, despite my efforts to clear them and fasten the guilt upon three of the most respectable and worthy citizens of Ghost Rock, convicted on the clearest proof. The murder would now be as wanton and reasonless as I could wish.

"One morning I shouldered my Winchester rifle, and going over to my uncle's house, near Nigger Head, asked my Aunt Mary, his wife, if he were at home, adding that I had come to kill him. My aunt replied with a peculiar smile that so many gentlemen called on the same errand

and were afterward carried away without having performed it, that I must excuse her for doubting my good faith in the matter. She said I did not look as if I would kill anybody, so, as a guarantee of good faith, I leveled my rifle and wounded a Chinaman who happened to be passing the house. She said she knew whole families who could do a thing of that kind, but Bill Ridley was a horse of another color. She said, however, that I would find him over on the other side of the creek in the sheep lot; and she added that she hoped the best man would win.

"My Aunt Mary was one of the most fair-minded women whom I have ever met.

"I found my uncle down on his knees engaged in skinning a sheep. Seeing that he had neither gun nor pistol handy, I had not the heart to shoot him, so I approached him, greeted him pleasantly, and struck him a powerful blow on the head with the butt of my rifle. I have a very good delivery, and Uncle William lay down on his side, then rolled over on his back, spread out his fingers, and shivered. Before he could recover the use of his limbs I seized the knife that he had been using and cut his hamstrings. You know, doubtless, that when you sever the *tendon Achillis* the patient has no further use of his leg; it is just the same as if he had no leg. Well, I parted them both, and when he revived he was at my service. As soon as he comprehended the situation, he said:

" 'Samuel, you have got the drop on me, and can afford to be liberal about this thing. I have only one thing to ask of you, and that is that you carry me to the house and finish me in the bosom of my family.'

"I told him I thought that a pretty reasonable request, and I would do so if he would let me put him in a wheat sack; he would be easier to carry that way, and if we were seen by the neighbors *en route* it would cause less remark. He agreed to that, and going to the barn I got a sack. This, however, did not fit him; it was too short and much wider than he was; so I bent his legs, forced his knees up against his breast, and got him into it that way, tying the sack above his head. He was a heavy man, and I had all I could do to get him on my back, but I staggered along for some distance until I came to a swing which some of the children had suspended to the branch of the oak. Here I laid him down and sat upon him to rest, and the sight of the rope gave me a happy inspiration. In twenty minutes my uncle, still in the sack, swung free to the sport of the wind. I had taken down the rope, tied one end tightly about the mouth of the bag, thrown the other across the limb, and hauled him up about five feet from the ground. Fastening the other end of the rope also about the mouth of sack, I had the satisfaction to see my uncle converted into a huge pendulum. I must add that he was not himself entirely aware of the nature of the change which he had undergone in his relation to the exterior world, though in justice to a brave man's memory I ought to say that I do not think he would in any case have wasted much of my time in vain remonstrance.

"Uncle William had a ram which was famous in all that region as a fighter. It was in a state of chronic constitutional indignation. Some deep disappointment in early life had soured its disposition, and it had declared war upon the whole world. To say that it would butt anything accessible is but faintly to express the nature and scope of its military activity: the universe was its antagonist; its method was that of a projectile. It fought, like the angels and devils, in mid-air, cleaving the atmosphere like a bird, describing a parabolic curve and descending upon its victim at just the exact angle of incidence to make the most of its velocity and weight. Its momentum, calculated in foot-tons, was something incredible. It had been seen to destroy a four year old bull by a single impact upon that animal's gnarly forehead. No stone wall had ever been known to resist its downward swoop; there were no trees tough enough to stay it; it would splinter them into matchwood, and defile their leafy honors in the dust. This irascible and implacable brute—this incarnate thunderbolt —this monster of the upper deep, I had seen reposing in the shade of an adjacent tree, dreaming dreams of conquest and glory. It was with a view to summoning it forth to the field of honor that I suspended its master in the manner described.

"Having completed my preparations, I imparted to the avuncular pendulum a gentle oscillation, and retiring to cover behind a contiguous rock, lifted up my voice in a long, rasping cry whose diminishing final note was drowned in a noise like that of a swearing cat, which emanated from the sack. Instantly that formidable sheep was upon its feet and had taken in the military situation at a glance. In a few moments it had approached, stamping, to within fifty yards of the swinging foeman who, now retreating and anon advancing, seemed to invite the fray. Suddenly I saw the beast's head drop earthward as if depressed by the weight of its enormous horns; then a dim, white, wavy streak of sheep prolonged itself from that spot in a generally horizontal direction to within about four yards of a point immediately beneath the enemy. There it struck sharply upward, and before it had faded from my gaze at the place whence it had set out I heard a horrible thump and a piercing scream, and my poor uncle shot forward with a slack rope, higher than the limb to which he was attached. Here the rope tautened with a jerk, arresting this flight, and back he swung in a breathless curve to the other end of his arc. The ram had fallen, a heap of indistinguishable legs, wool, and horns, but, pulling himself together and dodging as its antagonist swept downward, it retired at random, alternately shaking its head and stamping its fore feet. When it had backed about the same distance as that from which it had delivered the assault it paused again, bowed its head as if in prayer for victory, and again shot forward, dimly visible as before—a prolonging white streak with monstrous undulations, ending with a sharp ascension. Its course this time was at a right angle to its former one, and its impatience so great that it struck the enemy before he had nearly reached the lowest point of his arc. In consequence he went flying around and around in a horizontal circle, whose radius was about equal to half the length of the rope, which I forgot to say was nearly twenty feet long. His shrieks, *crescendo* in approach and *diminuendo* in recession, made the rapidity of his revolution more obvious to the ear than to the eye. He had evidently not yet been struck in a vital spot. His posture in the sack and the distance from the ground at which he hung compelled the ram to operate upon his lower extremities and the end of his back. Like a plant that has struck its root into some poisonous mineral, my poor uncle was dying slowly upward.

"After delivering its second blow the ram had not again retired. The fever of battle burned hot in its heart; its brain was intoxicated with the wine of strife. Like a pugilist who in his rage forgets his skill and fights ineffectively at half-arm's length, the angry beast endeavored to reach its fleeting foe by awkward vertical leaps as he passed overhead, sometimes, indeed, succeeding in striking him feebly, but more frequently overthrown by its own misguided eagerness. But as the impetus was exhausted and the man's circle narrowed in scope and diminished in speed, bringing him nearer to the ground, these tactics produced better results and elicited a superior quality of screams, which I greatly enjoyed.

"Suddenly, as if the bugles had sung truce, the ram suspended hostilities and walked away, thoughtfully wrinkling and smoothing its great aquiline nose, and occasionally cropping a bunch of grass and slowly munching it. It seemed to have tired of war's alarms and resolved to beat the sword into a plowshare and cultivate the arts of peace. Steadily it held its course away from the field of fame until it had gained a distance of nearly a quarter of a mile. There it stopped and stood with its rear to the foe, chewing its cud and apparently half asleep. I observed, however, an occasional slight turn of its head, as if its apathy were more affected than real.

"Meantime Uncle William's shrieks had abated with his

motion, and nothing was heard from him but long, low moans, and at long intervals my name, uttered in pleading tones exceedingly grateful to my ear. Evidently the man had not the faintest notion of what was being done to him, and was inexpressibly terrified. When Death comes cloaked in mystery he is terrible indeed. Little by little my uncle's oscillations diminished, and finally he hung motionless. I went to him and was about to give him the *coup de grâce,* when I heard and felt a succession of smart shocks which shook the ground like a series of light earthquakes, and turning in the direction of the ram, saw a long cloud of dust approaching me with inconceivable rapidity and alarming effect. At a distance of some thirty yards away it stopped short, and from the near end of it rose into the air what I at first thought a great white bird. Its ascent was so smooth and easy and regular that I could not realize its extraordinary celerity, and was lost in admiration of its grace. To this day the impression remains that it was a slow, deliberate movement, the ram—for it was that animal—being upborne by some power other than its own impetus, and supported through the successive stages of its flight with infinite tenderness and care. My eyes followed its progress through the air with unspeakable pleasure, all the greater by contrast with my former terror of its approach by land. Onward and upward the noble animal sailed, its head bent down almost between its knees, its fore feet thrown back, its hinder legs trailing to rear like the legs of a soaring heron. At a height of forty or fifty feet, as nearly as I could judge, it attained its zenith and appeared to remain an instant stationary; then, tilting suddenly forward without altering the relative position of its parts, it shot downward on a steeper and steeper course with augmenting velocity, passed immediately above me with a noise like the rush of a cannon shot, and struck my poor uncle almost squarely on the top of the head! So frightful was the impact that not only the neck was broken, but the rope too; and the body of the deceased, forced against the earth, was crushed to pulp beneath the awful front of that meteoric sheep! The concussion stopped all the clocks between Lone Hand and Dutch Dan's, and Professor Davidson, who happened to be in the vicinity, promptly explained that the vibrations were from north to south."

Altogether, I cannot help thinking that in point of atrocity my murder of Uncle William has seldom been excelled.

The Clock
William Fryer Harvey

*I think that for sheer menace this is
the most powerful story I have ever
read, though exactly what it is that
is menacing, and exactly what it is
menacing to do are entirely mysterious.
Perhaps you can figure it out,
but I hope, for your sake, that you can't.*

I LIKED your description of the people at the *pension*. I can just picture that rather sinister Miss Cornelius, with her toupee and clinking bangles. I don't wonder you felt frightened that night when you found her sleep-walking in the corridor. But after all, why shouldn't she sleep-walk? As to the movements of the furniture in the lounge on the Sunday, you are, I suppose, in an earthquake zone, though an earthquake seems too big an explanation for the ringing of that little handbell on the mantelpiece. It's rather as if our parlormaid—another new one!—were to call a stray elephant to account for the teapot we found broken yesterday. You have at least escaped the eternal problem of maids in Italy.

Yes, my dear, I most certainly believe you. I have never had experiences quite like yours, but your mention of Miss Cornelius has reminded me of something rather similar that happened nearly twenty years ago, soon after I left school. I was staying with my aunt in Hampstead. You remember her, I expect; or, if not her, the poodle, Monsieur, that she used to make perform such pathetic tricks. There was another guest, whom I had never met before, a Mrs. Caleb. She lived in Lewes and had been staying with my aunt for about a fortnight, recuperating after a series of domestic upheavals, which had culminated in her two servants leaving her at an hour's notice, without any reason, according to Mrs. Caleb; but I wondered. I had never seen the maids; I had seen Mrs Caleb and, frankly, I disliked her. She left the same sort of impression on me as I gather your Miss Cornelius leaves on you—something queer and secretive; underground, if you can use the expression, rather than underhand. And I could feel in my body that she did not like me.

It was summer. Joan Denton—you remember her; her husband was killed in Gallipoli—had suggested that I should go down to spend the day with her. Her people had rented a little cottage some three miles out of Lewes. We arranged a day. It was gloriously fine for a wonder, and I had planned to leave that stuffy old Hampstead house before the old ladies were astir. But Mrs. Caleb waylaid me in the hall, just as I was going out.

'I wonder,' she said, 'I wonder if you could do me a small favor. If you *do* have any time to spare in Lewes—only if you do—would you be so kind as to call at my house? I left a little travelling-clock there in the hurry of parting. If it's not in the drawing-room, it will be in my bedroom or in one of the maids' bedrooms. I know I lent it to the cook, who was a poor riser, but I can't remember if she returned it. Would it be too much to ask? The house has been locked up for twelve days, but everything is in order. I have the keys here; the large one is for the garden gate, the small one for the front door.'

I could only accept, and she proceeded to tell me how I could find Ash Grove House.

'You will feel quite like a burglar,' she said. 'But mind, it's only if you have time to spare.'

As a matter of fact I found myself glad of any excuse to kill time. Poor old Joan had been taken suddenly ill in the night—they feared appendicitis—and though her people were very kind and asked me to stay to lunch, I could see that I should only be in the way, and made Mrs. Caleb's commission an excuse for an early departure.

I found Ash Grove without difficulty. It was a medium-sized red-brick house, standing by itself in a high-walled garden that bounded a narrow lane. A flagged path led from the gate to the front door, in front of which grew, not an ash, but a monkey-puzzle, that must have made the rooms unnecessarily gloomy. The side door, as I expected, was locked. The dining-room and drawing-room lay on either side of the hall and, as the windows of both were shuttered, I left the hall door open, and in the dim light looked round hurriedly for the clock, which, from what Mrs. Caleb had said, I hardly expected to find in either of the downstairs rooms: It was neither on table nor mantelpiece. The rest of the furniture was carefully covered over with white dust-sheets. Then I went upstairs. But, before doing so, I closed the front door. I did in fact feel rather like a burglar, and I thought that if any one did happen to see the front door open, I might have difficulty in explaining things. Happily the upstairs windows were not shuttered. I made a hurried search of the principal bedrooms. They had been left in apple-pie order; nothing was out of place; but there was no sign of Mrs. Caleb's clock. The impression that the house gave me—you know the sense of personality that a house conveys—was neither pleasing nor displeasing, but it was stuffy, stuffy from the absence of fresh air, with an additional stuffiness added, that seemed to come out from the hangings and quilts and antimacassars. The corridor, on to which the bedrooms I had examined opened, communicated with a smaller wing, an older part of the house, I imagined, which contained a box-room and the maids' sleeping quarters. The last door that I unlocked—(I should say that the doors of all the rooms were locked, and relocked by me after I had glanced inside them)—contained the object of my search. Mrs. Caleb's travelling-clock was on the mantelpiece, ticking away merrily.

That was how I thought of it at first. And then for the first time I realized that there was something wrong. The clock had no business to be ticking. The house had been shut up for twelve days. No one had come in to air it or light fires. I remembered how Mrs. Caleb had told my aunt that if she left the keys with a neighbor, she was never sure who might get hold of them. And yet the clock was going. I wondered if some vibration had set the mechanism in motion, and pulled out my watch to see the time. It was five minutes to one. The clock on the mantelpiece said four minutes to the hour. Then, without quite knowing why, I shut the door on the landing, locked myself in, and again looked round the room. Nothing was out of place. The only thing that might have called for remark was that there appeared to be a slight indentation on the pillow and the bed; but the mattress was a feather mattress, and you know how difficult it is to make them perfectly smooth. You won't need to be told that I gave a hurried glance under the bed—do you remember your supposed burglar in Number Six at St. Ursula's?—and then, and much more reluctantly, opened the doors of two horribly capacious cupboards, both happily empty, except for a framed text with its face to the wall. By this time I really was frightened. The clock went ticking on. I had a horrible feeling that an alarm might go off at any moment, and the thought of being in that empty house was almost too much for me. However, I made an attempt to pull myself together. It might after all be a fourteen-day clock. If it were, then it would be almost run down. I could roughly find out how long the clock had been going by winding it up. I hesitated to put the matter to the test; but the uncertainty was too much for me. I took it out of is case and began to wind. I had scarcely turned the winding-screw twice when it stopped. The clock clearly was not running down; the hands had been set in motion probably only an hour or two before. I felt cold and faint

and, going to the window, threw up the sash, letting in the
sweet, live air of the garden. I knew now that the house
was queer, horribly queer. Could someone be living in the
house? Was someone else in the house now? I thought
that I had been in all the rooms, but had I? I had only
just opened the bath-room door, and I had certainly not
opened any cupboards, except those in the room in which
I was. Then, as I stood by the open window, wondering
what I should do next and feeling that I just couldn't go
down that corridor into the darkened hall to fumble at the
latch of the front door with I don't know what behind me,
I heard a noise. It was very faint at first, and seemed to
be coming from the stairs. It was a curious noise—not the
noise of any one climbing up the stairs, but—you will
laugh if this letter reaches you by a morning post—of
something hopping up the stairs, like a very big bird
would hop. I heard it on the landing; it stopped. Then
there was a curious scratching noise against one of the
bedroom doors, the sort of noise you can make with the
nail of your little finger scratching polished wood. Whatever it was, was coming slowly down the corridor,
scratching at the doors as it went. I could stand it no longer. Nightmare pictures of locked doors opening filled my
brain. I took up the clock, wrapped it in my mackintosh,
and dropped it out of the window on a flower-bed. Then I
managed to crawl out of the window and, getting a grip of
the sill, 'successfully negotiated,' as the journalists would
say, 'a twelve-foot drop.' So much for our much abused
gym at St. Ursula's. Picking up the mackintosh, I ran
round to the front door and locked it. Then I felt I could
breathe, but not until I was on the far side of the gate in
the garden wall did I feel safe.

Then I remembered that the bedroom window was
open. What was I to do? Wild horses wouldn't have
dragged me into that house again unaccompanied. I made
up my mind to go to the police-station and tell them everything. I should be laughed at, of course, and they
might easily refuse to believe my story of Mrs. Caleb's

commission. I had actually begun to walk down the lane in the direction of the town, when I chanced to look back at the house. The window that I had left open was shut.

No, my dear, I didn't see any face or anything dreadful like that . . . and, of course, it may have shut by itself. It was an ordinary sash-window, and you know they are often difficult to keep open.

And the rest? Why, there's really nothing more to tell. I didn't even see Mrs. Caleb again. She had had some sort of fainting fit just before lunch-time, my aunt informed me on my return, and had had to go to bed. Next morning I travelled down to Cornwall to join mother and the children. I thought I had forgotten all about it, but when three years later Uncle Charles suggested giving me a travelling-clock for a twenty-first birthday present, I was foolish enough to prefer the alternative that he offered, a collected edition of the works of Thomas Carlyle.

The Harbor-Master

Robert W. Chambers

*The evocation of the sheer physical presence
of a monster has never, I think, been better
done, and I wager you'll wince when you come
in contact with it. My guess is that this story
was the result of a particularly nasty dream.*

Where the slanting forest eaves,
Shingled tight with greenest leaves,
Sweep the scented meadow-sedge,
Let us snoop along the edge;
Let us pry in hidden nooks,
Laden with our nature books,
Scaring birds with happy cries,
Chloroforming butterflies,
Rooting up each woodland plant,
Pinning beetle, fly, and ant,
So we may identify
What we've ruined, by-and-by.

ECAUSE it all seems so improbable—
so horribly impossible to me now, sitting here safe and
sane in my own library—I hesitate to record an episode
which already appears to me less horrible than grotesque.
Yet, unless this story is written now, I know I shall never
have the courage to tell the truth about the matter—not

from fear of ridicule, but because I myself shall soon cease to credit what I now know to be true. Yet scarcely a month has elapsed since I heard the stealthy purring of what I believed to be the shoaling undertow—scarcely a month ago, with my own eyes, I saw that which, even now, I am beginning to believe never existed. As for the harbor-master—and the blow I am now striking at the old order of things— But of that I shall not speak now, or later; I shall try to tell the story simply and truthfully, and let my friends testify as to my probity and the publishers of this book corroborate them.

On the 29th of February I resigned my position under the government and left Washington to accept an offer from Professor Farrago—whose name he kindly permits me to use—and on the first day of April I entered upon my new and congenial duties as general superintendent of the water-fowl department connected with the Zoological Gardens then in course of erection at Bronx Park, New York.

For a week I followed the routine, examining the new foundations, studying the architect's plans, following the surveyors through the Bronx thickets, suggesting arrangements for water-courses and pools destined to be included in the enclosures for swans, geese, pelicans, herons, and such of the waders and swimmers as we might expect to acclimate in Bronx Park.

It was at that time the policy of the trustees and officers of the Zoological Gardens neither to employ collectors not to send out expeditions in search of specimens. The society decided to depend upon voluntary contributions, and I was always busy, part of the day, in dictating answers to correspondents who wrote offering their services as hunters of big game, collectors of all sorts of fauna, trappers, snarers, and also to those who offered specimens for sale, usually at exorbitant rates.

To the proprietors of five-legged kittens, mangy lynxes, moth-eaten coyotes, and dancing bears I returned courteous but uncompromising refusals—of course, first submitting all such letters, together with my replies, to Professor Farrago.

One day towards the end of May, however, just as I was leaving Bronx Park to return to town, Professor Lesard, of the reptilian department, called out to me that Professor Farrago wanted to see me a moment; so I put my pipe into my pocket again and retraced my steps to the temporary, wooden building occupied by Professor Farrago, general superintendent of the Zoological Gardens. The professor, who was sitting at his desk before a pile of letters and replies submitted for approval by me, pushed his glasses down and looked over them at me with a whimsical smile that suggested amusement, impatience, annoyance, and perhaps a faint trace of apology.

"Now, here's a letter," he said, with a deliberate gesture towards a sheet of paper impaled on a file—"a letter that I suppose you remember." He disengaged the sheet of paper and handed it to me.

"Oh yes," I replied, with a shrug; "of course the man is mistaken—or—"

"Or what?" demanded Professor Farrago, tranquilly, wiping his glasses.

"—Or a liar," I replied.

After a silence he leaned back in his chair and bade me read the letter to him again, and I did so with a contemptuous tolerance for the writer, who must have been either a very innocent victim or a very stupid swindler. I said as much to Professor Farrago, but, to my surprise, he appeared to waver.

"I suppose," he said, with his near-sighted, embarrassed smile, "that nine hundred and ninety-nine men in a thousand would throw that letter aside and condemn the writer as a liar or a fool?"

"In my opinion," said I, "he's one or the other."

"He isn't—in mine," said the professor, placidly.

"What!" I exclaimed. "Here is a man living all alone on a strip of rock and sand between the wilderness and the sea, who wants you to send somebody to take charge of a bird that doesn't exist!"

"How do you know," asked Professor Farrago, "that the bird in question does not exist?"

"It is generally accepted," I replied, sarcastically, "that the great auk has been extinct for years. Therefore I may be pardoned for doubting that our correspondent possesses a pair of them alive."

"Oh, you young fellows," said the professor, smiling wearily, "you embark on a theory for destinations that don't exist."

He leaned back in his chair, his amused eyes searching space for the imagery that made him smile.

"Like swimming squirrels, you navigate with the help of Heaven and a stiff breeze, but you never land where you hope to—do you?"

Rather red in the face, I said: "Don't you believe the great auk to be extinct?"

"Audubon saw the greak auk."

"Who has seen a single specimen since?"

"Nobody—except our correspondent here," he replied, laughing.

I laughed, too, considering the interview at an end, but the professor went on, coolly:

"Whatever it is that our correspondent has—and I am daring to believe that it *is* the great auk itself—I want you to secure it for the society."

When my astonishment subsided my first conscious sentiment was one of pity. Clearly, Professor Farrago was on the verge of dotage—ah, what a loss to the world!

I believe now that Professor Farrago perfectly interpreted my thoughts, but he betrayed neither resentment nor impatience. I drew a chair up beside his desk—there was nothing to do but to obey, and this fool's errand was none of my conceiving.

Together we made out a list of articles necessary for me and itemized the expenses I might incur, and I set a date for my return, allowing no margin for a successful termination to the expedition.

"Never mind that," said the professor. "What I want you to do is to get those birds here safely. Now, how many men will you take?"

"None," I replied, bluntly; "it's a useless expense, unless there is something to bring back. If there is I'll wire you, you may be sure."

"Very well," said Professor Farrago, good-humoredly, "you shall have all the assistance you may require. Can you leave to-night?"

The old gentleman was certainly prompt. I nodded, half-sulkily, aware of his amusement.

"So," I said, picking up my hat, "I am to start north to find a place called Black Harbor, where there is a man named Halyard who possesses, among other household utensils, two extinct great auks——"

We were both laughing by this time. I asked him why on earth he credited the assertion of a man he had never before heard of.

"I suppose," he replied, with the same half-apologetic, half-humorous smile, "it is instinct. I feel, somehow, that this man Halyard *has* got an auk—perhaps two. I can't get away from the idea that we are on the eve of acquiring the rarest of living creatures. It's odd for a scientist to talk as I do; doubtless you're shocked—admit it, now!"

But I was not shocked; on the contrary, I was conscious that the same strange hope that Professor Farrago cherished was beginning, in spite of me, to stir my pulses, too.

"If he has——" I began, then stopped.

The professor and I looked hard at each other in silence.

"Go on," he said, encouragingly.

But I had nothing more to say, for the prospect of beholding with my own eyes a living specimen of the great auk produced a series of conflicting emotions within me which rendered speech profanely superfluous.

As I took my leave Professor Farrago came to the door of the temporary, wooden office and handed me the letter written by the man Halyard. I folded it and put it into my pocket, as Halyard might require it for my own identification.

"How much does he want for the pair?" I asked.

"Ten thousand dollars. Don't demur—if the birds are really—"

"I know," I said, hastily, not daring to hope too much.

"One thing more," said Professor Farrago, gravely; "you know, in that last paragraph of his letter, Halyard speaks of something else in the way of specimens—an undiscovered species of amphibious biped—just read that paragraph again, will you?"

I drew the letter from my pocket and read as he directed:

When you have seen the two living specimens of the great auk, and have satisfied yourself that I tell the truth, you may be wise enough to listen without prejudice to a statement I shall make concerning the existence of the strangest creature ever fashioned. I will merely say, at this time, that the creature referred to is an amphibious biped and inhabits the ocean near this coast. More I cannot say, for I personally have not seen the animal, but I have a witness who has, and there are many who affirm that they have seen the creature. You will naturally say that my statement amounts to nothing; but when your representative arrives, if he be free from prejudice, I expect his reports to you concerning this sea-biped will confirm the solemn statements of a witness I *know* to be unimpeachable.

Yours truly, BURTON HALYARD.

BLACK HARBOR.

"Well," I said, after a moment's thought, "here goes for the wild-goose chase."

"Wild auk, you mean," said Professor Farrago, shaking hands with me. "You will start to-night, won't you?"

"Yes, but Heaven knows how I'm ever going to land in this man Halyard's door-yard. Good-bye!"

"About that sea-biped—" began Professor Farrago, shyly.

"Oh, don't!" I said; "I can swallow the auks, feathers and claws, but if this fellow Halyard is hinting he's seen an amphibious creature resembling a man—"

"—Or a woman," said the professor, cautiously.

I retired, disgusted, my faith shaken in the mental vigor of Professor Farrago.

II

THE three days' voyage by boat and rail was irksome. I bought my kit at Sainte Croix, on the Central Pacific Railroad, and on June 1st I began the last stage of my journey *via* the Sainte Isole broad-gauge, arriving in the wilderness by daylight. A tedious forced march by blazed trail, freshly spotted on the wrong side, of course, brought me to the northern terminus of the rusty, narrow-gauge lumber railway which runs from the heart of the hushed pine wilderness to the sea.

Already a long train of battered flat-cars, piled with sluice-props and roughly hewn sleepers, was moving slowly off into the brooding forest gloom, when I came in sight of the track; but I developed a gratifying and unexpected burst of speed, shouting all the while. The train stopped; I swung myself aboard the last car, where a pleasant young fellow was sitting on the rear brake, chewing spruce and reading a letter.

"Come aboard, sir," he said, looking up with a smile; "I guess you're the man in a hurry."

"I'm looking for a man named Halyard," I said, dropping rifle and knapsack on the fresh-cut, fragrant pile of pine. "Are you Halyard?"

"No, I'm Francis Lee, bossing the mica. pit at Port-of-Waves," he replied, "but this letter is from Halyard, asking me to look out for a man in a hurry from Bronx Park, New York."

"I'm that man," said I, filling my pipe and offering him a share of the weed of peace, and we sat side by side smoking very amiably, until a signal from the locomotive sent him forward and I was left alone, lounging at ease, head pillowed on both arms, watching the blue sky flying through the branches overhead.

Long before we came in sight of the ocean I smelled it; the fresh, salt aroma stole into my senses, drowsy with the heated odor of pine and hemlock, and I sat up, peering ahead into the dusky sea of pines.

Fresher and fresher came the wind from the sea, in puffs, in mild, sweet breezes, in steady, freshening currents, blowing the feathery crowns of the pines, setting the balsam's blue tufts rocking.

Lee wandered back over the long line of flats, balancing himself nonchalantly as the cars swung around a sharp curve, where water dripped from a newly propped sluice that suddenly emerged from the depths of the forest to run parallel to the railroad track.

"Built in this spring," he said, surveying his handiwork, which seemed to undulate as the cars swept past. "It runs to the cove—or ought to—" He stopped abruptly with a thoughtful glance at me.

"So you're going over to Halyard's?" he continued, as though answering a question asked by himself.

I nodded.

"You've never been there—of course?"

"No," I said, "and I'm not likely to go again."

I would have told him why I was going if I had not already begun to feel ashamed of my idiotic errand.

"I guess you're going to look at those birds of his," continued Lee, placidly.

"I guess I am," I said, sulkily, glancing askance to see whether he was smiling.

But he only asked me, quite seriously, whether a great auk was really a very rare bird; and I told him that the

last one even seen had been found dead off Labrador in
January, 1870. Then I asked him whether these birds of
Halyard's were really great auks, and he replied, some-
what indifferently, that he supposed they were—at least,
nobody had ever before seen such birds near Port-of-
Waves.

"There's something else," he said, running a pine-sliver
through his pipe-stem—"something that interests us all
here more than auks, big or little. I suppose I might as
well speak of it, as you are bound to hear about it sooner
or later."

He hesitated, and I could see that he was embarrassed,
searching for the exact words to convey his meaning.

"If," said I, "you have anything in this region more
important to science than the great auk, I should be very
glad to know about it."

Perhaps there was the faintest tinge of sarcasm in my
voice, for he shot a sharp glance at me and then turned
slightly. After a moment, however, he put his pipe into
his pocket, laid hold of the brake with both hands, vault-
ed to his perch aloft, and glanced down at me.

"Did you ever hear of the harbor-master?" he asked,
maliciously.

"Which harbor-master?" I inquired.

"You'll know before long," he observed, with a satisfied glance into perspective.

This rather extraordinary observation puzzled me. I
waited for him to resume, and, as he did not, I asked him
what he meant.

"If I knew," he said, "I'd tell you. But, come to think
of it, I'd be a fool to go into details with a scientific man.
You'll hear about the harbor-master—perhaps you will
see the harbor-master. In that event I should be glad to
converse with you on the subject."

I could not help laughing at his prim and precise manner, and after a moment, he also laughed, saying:

"It hurts a man's vanity to know he knows a thing that
somebody else knows he doesn't know. I'm damned if I

say another word about the harbor-master until you've been to Halyard's!"

"A harbor-master," I persisted, "is an official who superintends the mooring of ships—isn't he?"

But he refused to be tempted into conversation, and we lounged silently on the lumber until a long, thin whistle from the locomotive and a rush of stinging salt-wind brought us to our feet. Through the trees I could see the bluish-black ocean, stretching out beyond black headlands to meet the clouds; a great wind was roaring among the trees as the train slowly came into a stand-still on the edge of the primeval forest.

Lee jumped to the ground and aided me with my rifle and pack, and then the train began to back away along a curved side-track which, Lee said, led to the mica-pit and company stores.

"Now what will you do?" he asked, pleasantly. "I can give you a good dinner and a decent bed to-night if you like—and I'm sure Mrs. Lee would be very glad to have you stop with us as long as you choose."

I thanked him, but said that I was anxious to reach Halyard's before dark, and he very kindly led me along the cliffs and pointed out the path.

"This man Halyard," he said, "is an invalid. He lives at a cove called Black Harbor, and all his truck goes through to him over the company's road. We receive it here, and sent a pack-mule through once a month. I've met him; he's a bad-tempered hypochondriac, a cynic at heart, and a man whose word is never doubted. If he says he has a great auk, you may be satisfied he has."

My heart was beating with excitement at the prospect; I looked out across the wooded headlands and tangled stretches of dune and hollow, trying to realize what it might mean to me, to Professor Farrago, to the world, if I should lead back to New York a live auk.

"He's a crank," said Lee; "frankly, I don't like him. If you find it unpleasant there, come back to us."

"Does Halyard live alone?" I asked.

"Yes—except for a professional trained nurse—poor thing!"

"A man?"

"No," said Lee, disgustedly.

Presently he gave me a peculiar glance; hesitated, and finally said: "Ask Halyard to tell you about his nurse and—the harbor-master. Good-bye—I'm due at the quarry. Come and stay with us whenever you care to; you will find a welcome at Port-of-Waves."

We shook hands and parted on the cliff, he turning back into the forest along the railway, I starting northward, pack slung, rifle over my shoulder. Once I met a group of quarrymen, faces burned brick-red, scarred hands swinging as they walked. And, as I passed them with a nod, turning, I saw that they also had turned to look after me, and I caught a word or two of their conversation, whirled back to me on the sea-wind.

They were speaking of the harbor-master.

III

Towards sunset I came out on a sheer granite cliff where the seabirds were whirling and clamoring, and the great breakers dashed, rolling in double-thundered reverberations on the sun-dyed, crimson sands below the rock.

Across the half-moon of beach towered another cliff, and, behind this, I saw a column of smoke rising in the still air. It certainly came from Halyard's chimney, although the opposite cliff prevented me from seeing the house itself.

I rested a moment to refill my pipe, then resumed rifle and pack, and cautiously started to skirt the cliffs. I had descended half-way towards the beach, and was examining the cliff opposite, when something on the very top of the rock arrested my attention—a man darkly outlined against the sky. The next moment, however, I knew it could not be a man, for the object suddenly glided over the face of the cliff and slid down the sheer, smooth face like a lizard. Before I could get a square look at it, the thing crawled into the surf—or, at least, it seemed to—but the whole episode occurred so suddenly, so unexpectedly, that I was not sure I had seen anything at all.

However, I was curious enough to climb the cliff on the land side and make my way towards the spot where I imagined I saw the man. Of course, there was nothing there—not a trace of a human being, I mean. Something *ha*d been there—a sea-otter, possibly—for the remains of a freshly killed fish lay on the rock, eaten to the backbone and tail.

The next moment, below me, I saw the house, a freshly painted trim, flimsy structure, modern, and very much out of harmony with the splendid savagery surrounding it. It struck a nasty, cheap note in the noble, grey monotony of headland and sea.

The descent was easy enough. I crossed the crescent beach, hard as pink marble, and found a little trodden path among the rocks, that led to the front porch of the house.

There were two people on the porch—I heard their voices before I saw them—and when I set my foot upon the wooden steps, I saw one of them, a woman, rise from her chair and step hastily towards me.

"Come back!" cried the other, a man with a smooth-shaven, deeply lined face, and a pair of angry, blue eyes; and the woman stepped back quietly, acknowledging my lifted hat with a silent inclination.

The man, who was reclining in an invalid's rolling-chair, clapped both large, pale hands to the wheels and pushed himself out along the porch. He had shawls pinned about him, an untidy, drab-colored hat on his head, and, when he looked down at me, he scowled.

"I know who you are," he said, in his acid voice; "you're one of the Zoological men from Bronx Park. You look like it, anyway."

"It is easy to recognize you from your reputation," I replied irritated at his discourtesy.

"Really," he replied, with something between a sneer and a laugh, "I'm obliged for your frankness. You're after my great auks, are you not?"

"Nothing else would have tempted me into this place," I replied, sincerely.

"Thank Heaven for that," he said. "Sit down a moment; you've interrupted us." Then, turning to the young woman, who wore the neat gown and tiny cap of a professional nurse, he bade her resume what she had been saying. She did so, with a deprecating glance at me, which made the old man sneer again.

"It happened so suddenly," she said, in her low voice, "that I had no chance to get back. The boat was drifting in the cove; I sat in the stern, reading, both oars shipped, and the tiller swinging. Then I heard a scratching under the boat, but thought it might be seaweed—and, next moment, came those soft thumpings, like the sound of a big fish rubbing its nose against a float."

Halyard clutched the wheels of his chair and stared at the girl in grim displeasure.

"Didn't you know enough to be frightened?" he demanded.

"No—not then," she said, coloring faintly; "but when, after a few moments, I looked up and saw the harbormaster running up and down the beach, I was horribly frightened."

"Really?" said Halyard, sarcastically; "it was about time." Then, turning to me, he rasped out: "And that young lady was obliged to row all the way to Port-of-Waves and call to Lee's quarrymen to take her boat in."

Completely mystified, I looked from Halyard to the girl, not in the least comprehending what all this meant.

"That will do," said Halyard, ungraciously, which curt phrase was apparently the usual dismissal for the nurse.

She rose, and I rose, and she passed me with an inclination, stepping noiselessly into the house.

"I want beef-tea!" bawled Halyard after her; then he gave me an unamiable glance.

"I was a well-bred man," he sneered; "I'm a Harvard graduate, too, but I live as I like, and I do what I like, and I say what I like."

"You certainly are not reticent," I said, disgusted.

"Why should I be?" he rasped; "I pay that young woman for my irritability; it's a bargain between us."

"In your domestic affairs," I said, "there is nothing that interests me. I came to see those auks."

"You probably believe them to be razor-billed auks," he said, contemptuously. "But they're not; they're great auks."

I suggested that he permit me to examine them, and he replied, indifferently, that they were in a pen in his backyard, and that I was free to step around the house when I cared to.

I laid my rifle and pack on the veranda, and hastened off with mixed emotions, among which hope no longer predominated. No man in his senses would keep two such precious prizes in a pen in his backyard, I argued, and I was perfectly prepared to find anything from a puffin to a penguin in that pen.

I shall never forget, as long as I live, my stupor of amazement when I came to the wire-covered enclosure. Not only were there two great auks in the pen, alive, breathing, squatting in bulky majesty on their seaweed bed, but one of them was gravely contemplating two newly hatched chicks, all bill and feet, which nestled sedately at the edge of a puddle of salt-water, where some small fish were swimming.

For a while excitement blinded, nay, deafened me. I tried to realize that I was gazing upon the last individuals of an all but extinct race—the sole survivors of the gigantic auk, which, for thirty years, has been accounted an extinct creature.

I believe that I did not move muscle nor limb until the sun had gone down and the crowding darkness blurred my straining eyes and blotted the great, silent, bright-eyed birds from sight.

Even then I could not tear myself away from the enclosure; I listened to the strange, drowsy note of the male bird, the fainter responses of the female, the thin plaints of the chicks, huddling under her breast; I heard their flipper-like, embryotic wings beating sleepily as the birds stretched and yawned their beaks and clacked them, preparing for slumber.

"If you please," came a soft voice from the door, "Mr. Halyard awaits your company to dinner."

IV

I DINED well—or, rather, I might have enjoyed my dinner if Mr. Halyard had been eliminated; and the feast consisted exclusively of a joint of beef, the pretty nurse, and myself. She was exceedingly attractive—with a disturbing fashion of lowering her head and raising her dark eyes when spoken to.

As for Halyard, he was unspeakable, bundled up in his snuffy shawls, and making uncouth noises over his gruel. But it is only just to say that his table was worth sitting down to and his wine was sound as a bell.

"Yah!" he snapped, "I'm sick of this cursed soup—and I'll trouble you to fill my glass—"

"It is dangerous for you to touch claret," said the pretty nurse.

"I might as well die at dinner as anywhere," he observed.

"Certainly," said I, cheerfully passing the decanter, but he did not appear overpleased with the attention.

"I can't smoke, either," he snarled, hitching the shawls around until he looked like Richard the Third.

However, he was good enough to shove a box of cigars at me, and I took one and stood up, as the pretty nurse slipped past and vanished into the little parlor beyond.

We sat there for a while without speaking. He picked irritably at the bread-crumbs on the cloth, never glancing in my direction; and I, tired from my long foot-tour, lay back in my chair, silently appreciating one of the best cigars I ever smoked.

"Well," he rasped out at length, "what do you think of my auks—and my veracity?"

I told him that both were unimpeachable.

"Didn't they call me a swindler down there at your museum?" he demanded.

I admitted that I had heard the term applied. Then I made a clean breast of the matter, telling him that it was I who had doubted; that my chief, Professor Farrago, had sent me against my will, and that I was ready and glad to admit that he, Mr. Halyard, was a benefactor of the human race.

"Bosh!" he said. "What good does a confounded wobbly, bandy-toed bird do to the human race?"

But he was pleased, nevertheless; and presently he asked me, not unamiably, to punish his claret again.

"I'm done for," he said; "good things to eat and drink are no good to me. Some day I'll get mad enough to have a fit, and then—"

He paused to yawn.

"Then," he continued, "that little nurse of mine will drink up my claret and go back to civilization, where people are polite."

Somehow or other, in spite of the fact that Halyard was an old pig, what he had said touched me. There was certainly not much left in life for him—as he regarded life.

"I'm going to leave her this house," he said, arranging his shawls. "She doesn't know it. I'm going to leave her my money, too. She doesn't know that. Good Lord! What kind of a woman can she be to stand my bad temper for a few dollars a month!"

"I think," said I, "that it's partly because she's poor, partly because she's sorry for you."

He looked up with a ghastly smile.

"You think she really is sorry?"

Before I could answer he went on: "I'm no mawkish

sentimentalist, and I won't allow anybody to be sorry for me—do you hear?"

"Oh, I'm not sorry for you!" I said, hastily, and, for the first time since I had seen him, he laughed heartily, without a sneer.

We both seemed to feel better after that; I drank his wine and smoked his cigars, and he appeared to take a certain grim pleasure in watching me.

"There's no fool like a young fool," he observed, presently.

As I had no doubt he referred to me, I paid him no attention.

After fidgeting with his shawls, he gave me an oblique scowl and asked me my age.

"Twenty-four," I replied.

"Sort of a tadpole, aren't you?" he said.

As I took no offence, he repeated the remark.

"Oh, come," said I, "there's no use in trying to irritate me. I see through you; a row acts like a cocktail on you—but you'll have to stick to gruel in my company."

"I call that impudence!" he rasped out, wrathfully.

"I don't care what you call it," I replied, undisturbed, "I am not going to be worried by you. Anyway," I ended, "it is my opinion that you could be very good company if you chose."

The proposition appeared to take his breath away—at least, he said nothing more; and I finished my cigar in peace and tossed the stump into a saucer.

"Now," said I, "what price do you set upon your birds, Mr. Halyard?"

"Ten thousand dollars," he snapped, with an evil smile.

"You will receive a certified check when the birds are delivered," I said, quietly.

"You don't mean to say that you agree to that outrageous bargain—and I won't take a cent less, either—Good Lord!—haven't you any spirit left?" he cried, half rising from his pile of shawls.

His piteous eagerness for a dispute sent me into laughter impossible to control, and he eyed me, mouth open, animosity rising visibly.

Then he seized the wheels of his invalid chair and trundled away, too mad to speak; and I strolled out into the parlor, still laughing.

The pretty nurse was there, sewing under a hanging lamp.

"If I am not indiscreet——" I began.

"Indiscretion is the better part of valor," said she, dropping her head but raising her eyes.

So I sat down with a frivolous smile peculiar to the appreciated.

"Doubtless," said I, "you are hemming a 'kerchief."

"Doubtless I am not," she said; "this is a night-cap for Mr. Halyard."

A mental vision of Halyard in a night-cap, very mad, nearly set me laughing again.

"Like the King of Yvetot, he wears his crown in bed," I said, flippantly.

"The King of Yvetot might have made that remark," she observed, re-threading her needle.

It was unpleasant to be reproved. How large and red and hot a man's ears feel.

To cool them, I strolled out to the porch; and, after a while, the pretty nurse came out, too, and sat down in a chair not far away. She probably regretted her lost opportunity to be flirted with.

"I have so little company—it is a great relief to see somebody from the world," she said. "If you can be agreeable, I wish you would."

The idea that she had come out to see me was so agreeable that I remained speechless until she said: "Do tell me what people are doing in New York."

So I seated myself on the steps and talked about the portion of the world inhabited by me, while she sat sewing in the dull light that straggled out from the parlor windows.

She had a certain coquetry of her own, using the usual

methods with an individuality that was certainly fetching. For instance, when she lost her needle—and, another time, when we both, on hands and knees, hunted for her thimble.

However, directions for these pastimes may be found in contemporary classics.

I was as entertaining as I could be—perhaps not quite as entertaining as a young man usually thinks he is. However, we got on very well together until I asked her tenderly who the harbor-master might be, whom they all discussed so mysteriously.

"I do not care to speak about it," she said, with a primness of which I had not suspected her capable.

Of course I could scarcely pursue the subject after that—and, indeed, I did not intend to—so I began to tell her how I fancied I had seen a man on the cliff that afternoon, and how the creature slid over the sheer rock like a snake.

To my amazement, she asked me to kindly discontinue the account of my adventures, in an icy tone, which left no room for protest.

"It was only a sea-otter," I tried to explain, thinking perhaps she did not care for snake stories.

But the explanation did not appear to interest her, and I was mortified to observe that my impression upon her was anything but pleasant.

"She doesn't seem to like me and my stories," thought I, "but she is too young, perhaps, to appreciate them."

So I forgave her—for she was even prettier than I had thought her at first—and I took my leave, saying that Mr. Halyard would doubtless direct me to my room.

Halyard was in his library, cleaning a revolver, when I entered.

"Your room is next to mine," he said; "pleasant dreams, and kindly refrain from snoring."

"May I venture an absurd hope that you will do the same!" I replied, politely.

That maddened him, so I hastily withdrew.

I had been asleep for at least two hours when a movement by my bedside and a light in my eyes awakened me. I sat bolt upright in bed, blinking at Halyard, who, clad in a dressing-gown and wearing a night-cap, had wheeled himself into my room with one hand, while with the other he solemnly waved a candle over my head.

"I'm so cursed lonely," he said—"come, there's a good fellow—talk to me in your own original, impudent way."

I objected strenuously, but he looked so worn and thin, so lonely and bad-tempered, so lovelessly grotesque, that I got out of bed and passed a spongeful of cold water over my head.

Then I returned to bed and propped the pillows up for a back-rest, ready to quarrel with him if it might bring some little pleasure into his morbid existence.

"No," he said, amiably, "I'm too worried to quarrel, but I'm much obliged for your kindly offer. I want to tell you something."

"What?" I asked, suspiciously.

"I want to ask you if you ever saw a man with gills like a fish?"

"Gills?" I repeated.

"Yes, gills! Did you?"

"No," I replied, angrily, "and neither did you."

"No, I never did," he said, in a curiously placid voice, "but there's a man with gills like a fish who lives in the ocean out there. Oh, you needn't look that way—nobody ever thinks of doubting my word, and I tell you that there's a man—or a thing that looks like a man—as big as you are, too——all slate-colored—with nasty red gills like a fish!—and I've a witness to prove what I say!"

"Who?" I asked, sarcastically.

"The witness? My nurse."

"Oh! She saw a slate-colored man with gills?"

"Yes, she did. So did Francis Lee, superintendent of the Mica Quarry Company at Port-of-Waves. So have a dozen men who work in the quarry. Oh, you needn't laugh, young man. It's an old story here, and anybody can tell you about the harbor-master."

"The harbor-master!" I exclaimed.

"Yes, that slate-colored thing with gills, that looks like a man—and—by Heaven! *is* a man—that's the harbor-master. Ask any quarryman at Port-of-Waves what it is that comes purring around their boats at the wharf and unties painters and changes the mooring of every cat-boat in the cove at night! Ask Francis Lee what it was he saw running and leaping up and down the shoal at sunset last Friday! Ask anybody along the coast what sort of a thing moves about the cliffs like a man and slides over them into the sea like an otter—"

"I saw it do that!" I burst out.

"Oh, did you? Well, *what was it?*"

Something kept me silent, although a dozen explanations flew to my lips.

After a pause. Halyard said: "You saw the harbor-master, that's what you saw!"

I looked at him without a word.

"Don't mistake me," he said, pettishly; "I don't think that the harbor-master is a spirit or a sprite or a hobgoblin, or any sort of damned rot. Neither do I believe it to be an optical illusion."

"What do you think it is?" I asked.

"I think it's a man—I think it's a branch of the human race—that's what I think. Let me tell you something: the deepest spot in the Atlantic Ocean is a trifle over five miles deep—and I suppose you know that this place lies only about a quarter of a mile off this headland. The British exploring vessel, *Gull,* Captain Marotte, discovered and sounded it, I believe. Anyway, it's there, and it's my belief that the profound depths are inhabited by the remnants of the last race of amphibious human beings!"

This was childish; I did not bother to reply.

"Believe it or not, as you will," he said, angrily; "one thing I know, and that is this: the harbor-master has taken to hanging around my cove, and he is attracted by my nurse! I won't have it! I'll blow his fishy gills out of his head if I ever get a shot at him! I don't care whether it's homicide or not—anyway, it's a new kind of murder and it attracts me!"

I gazed at him incredulously, but he was working himself into a passion, and I did not choose to say what I thought.

"Yes, this slate-colored thing with gills goes purring and grinning and spitting about after my nurse—when she walks, when she rows, when she sits on the beach! Gad! It drives me nearly frantic. I won't tolerate it, I tell you!"

"No," said I, "I wouldn't either." And I rolled over in bed convulsed with laughter.

The next moment I heard my door slam. I smothered my mirth and rose to close the window, for the land-wind blew cold from the forest, and a drizzle was sweeping the carpet as far as my bed.

That luminous glare which sometimes lingers after the stars go out, threw a trembling, nebulous radiance over sand and cove. I heard the seething currents under the breakers' softened thunder— louder than I ever heard it. Then, as I closed my window, lingering for a last look at the crawling tide, I saw a man standing, ankle-deep, in the surf, all alone there in the night. But—was it a man? For the figure suddenly began running over the beach on all fours like a beetle, waving its limbs like feelers. Before I could throw open the window again it darted into the surf, and, when I leaned out into the chilling drizzle, I saw nothing save the flat ebb crawling on the coast—I heard nothing save the purring of bubbles on seething sands.

V

It took me a week to perfect my arrangements for transporting the great auks, by water, to Port-of-Waves, where a lumber schooner was to be sent from Petite Sainte Isole, chartered by me for a voyage to New York.

I had constructed a cage made of osiers, in which my

auks were to squat until they arrived at Bronx Park. My
telegrams to Professor Farrago were brief. One merely
said "Victory!" Another explained that I wanted no assistance; and a third read: "Schooner chartered. Arrive
New York July 1st. Send furniture-van to foot of Bluff
Street."

My week as a guest of Mr. Halyard proved interesting.
I wrangled with that invalid to his heart's content, I
worked all day on my osier cage, I hunted the thimble in
the moonlight with the pretty nurse. We sometimes found
it.

As for the thing they called the harbor-master, I saw it
a dozen times, but always either at night or so far away
and so close to the sea that of course no trace of it remained when I reached the spot, rifle in hand.

I had quite made up my mind that the so-called harbor-master was a demented darky—wandered from,
Heavens knows where—perhaps shipwrecked and gone
mad from his sufferings. Still, it was far from pleasant to
know that the creature was strongly attracted by the
pretty nurse.

She, however, persisted in regarding the harbor-master
as a sea-creature; she earnestly affirmed that it had gills,
like a fish's gills, that it had a soft, fleshy hole for a
mouth, and its eyes were luminous and lidless and fixed.

"Besides," she said, with a shudder, "it's all slate color,
like a porpoise, and it looks as wet as a sheet of india-
rubber in a dissecting-room."

The day before I was to set sail with my auks in a cat-
boat bound for Port-of-Waves, Halyard trundled up to me
in his chair and announced his intention of going with me.

"Going where?" I asked.

"To Port-of-Waves and then to New York," he replied,
tranquilly.

I was doubtful, and my lack of cordiality hurt his
feelings.

"Oh, of course, if you need the sea-voyage—" I began.

"I don't; I need you," he said, savagely; "I need the
stimulus of our daily quarrel. I never disagreed so

pleasantly with anybody in my life; it agrees with me; I
am a hundred per cent better than I was last week."

I was inclined to resent this, but something in the
deep-lined face of the invalid softened me. Besides, I had
taken a hearty liking to the old pig.

"I don't want any mawkish sentiment about it," he
said, observing me closely; "I won't permit anybody to
feel sorry for me—do you understand?"

"I'll trouble you to use a different tone in addressing
me," I replied, hotly; "I'll feel sorry for you if I choose
to!" And our usual quarrel proceeded, to his deep satisfaction.

By six o'clock next evening I had Halyard's luggage
stowed away in the cat-boat, and the pretty nurse's effects
corded down, with the newly hatched auk-chicks in a
hat-box on top. She and I placed the osier cage aboard,
securing it firmly, and then, throwing tablecloths over the
auks' heads, we led those simple and dignified birds down
the path and across the plank at the little wooden pier.
Together we locked up the house, while Halyard stormed
at us both and wheeled himself furiously up and down the
beach below. At the last moment she forgot her thimble.
But we found it, I forget where.

"Come on!" shouted Halyard, waving his shawls furiously; "what the devil are you about up there?

He received our explanation with a sniff, and we
trundled him aboard without further ceremony.

"Don't run me across the plank like a steamer trunk!"
he shouted, as I shot him dexterously into the cock-pit.
But the wind was dying away, and I had no time to dispute with him then.

The sun was setting above the pine-clad ridge as our
sail flapped and partly filled, and I cast off, and began a
long tack, east by south, to avoid the spouting rocks on
our starboard bow.

The sea-birds rose in clouds as we swung across the
shoal, the black surf-ducks scuttered out to sea, the gulls
tossed their sun-tipped wings in the ocean, riding the roll-
ers like bits of froth.

Already we were sailing slowly out across that great hole in the ocean, five miles deep, the most profound sounding ever taken in the Atlantic. The presence of great heights or great depths, seen or unseen, always impresses the human mind—perhaps oppresses it. We were very silent; the sunlight stain on cliff and beach deepened to crimson, then faded into sombre purple bloom that lingered long after the rose-tint died out in the zenith.

Our progress was slow; at times, although the sail filled with the rising land breeze, we scarcely seemed to move at all.

"Of course," said the pretty nurse, "we couldn't be aground in the deepest hole in the Atlantic."

"Scarcely," said Halyard, sarcastically, "unless we're grounded on a whale."

"What's that soft thumping?" I asked. "Have we run afoul of a barrel or log?"

It was almost too dark to see, but I leaned over the rail and swept the water with my hand.

Instantly something smooth glided under it, like the back of a great fish, and I jerked my hand back to the tiller. At the same moment the whole surface of the water seemed to begin to purr, with a sound like the breaking of froth in a champagne-glass.

"What's the matter with you?" asked Halyard, sharply.

"A fish came up under my hand," I said; "a porpoise or something—"

With a low cry, the pretty nurse clasped my arm in both her hands.

"Listen!" she whispered. "It's purring around the boat."

"What the devil's purring?" shouted Halyard. "I won't have anything purring around me!"

At that moment, to my amazement, I saw that the boat had stopped entirely, although the sail was full and the small pennant fluttered from the mast-head. Something, too, was tugging at the rudder, twisting and jerking it until the tiller strained and creaked in my hand. All at once it snapped; the tiller swung useless and the boat whirled around, heeling in the stiffening wind, and drove shore-ward.

It was then that I, ducking to escape the boom, caught a glimpse of something ahead—something that a sudden wave seemed to toss on deck and leave there, wet and flapping—a man with round, fixed, fishy eyes, and soft, slaty skin.

But the horror of the thing were the two gills that swelled and relaxed spasmodically, emitting a rasping, purring sound—two gasping, blood-red gills, all fluted and scolloped and distended.

Frozen with amazement and repugnance, I stared at the creature; I felt the hair stirring on my head and the icy sweat on my forehead.

"It's the harbor-master!" screamed Halyard.

The harbor-master had gathered himself into a wet lump, squatting motionless in the bows under the mast; his lidless eyes were phosphorescent, like the eyes of living codfish. After a while I felt that either fright or disgust was going to strangle me where I sat, but it was only the arms of the pretty nurse clasped around me in a frenzy of terror.

There was not a fire-arm aboard that we could get at. Halyard's hand crept backward where a steel-shod boat-hook lay, and I also made a clutch at it. The next moment I had it in my hand, and staggered forward, but the boat was already tumbling shoreward among the breakers, and the next I knew the harbor-master ran at me like a colossal rat, just as the boat rolled over and over through the surf, spilling freight and passengers among the sea-weed-covered rocks.

When I came to myself I was thrashing about knee-deep in a rocky pool, blinded by the water and half suffo-cated, while under my feet, like a stranded porpoise, the harbor-master made the water boil in his efforts to upset me. But his limbs seemed soft and boneless; he had no nails, no teeth, and he bounced and thumped and flapped and splashed like a fish, while I rained blows on him with the boathook that sounded like blows on a football. And all the while his gills were blowing out and frothing, and purring, and his lidless eyes looked into mine, until, nauseated and trembling, I dragged myself back to the beach, where already the pretty nurse alternately wrung her hands and her petticoats in ornamental despair.

Beyond the cove, Halyard was bobbing up and down, afloat in his invalid's chair, trying to steer shoreward. He was the maddest man I ever saw.

"Have you killed that rubber-headed thing yet?" he roared.

"I can't kill it," I shouted, breathlessly. "I might as well try to kill a football!"

"Can't you punch a hole in it?" he bawled. "If I can only get at him—"

His words were drowned in a thunderous splashing, a roar of great, broad flippers beating the sea, and I saw the gigantic forms of my two great auks, followed by their chicks, blundering past in a shower of spray, driving headlong out into the ocean.

"Oh, Lord!" I said. "I can't stand that," and, for the first time in my life, I fainted peacefully—and appropriately—at the feet of the pretty nurse.

It is within the range of possibility that this story may be doubted. It doesn't matter; nothing can add to the despair of a man who has lost two great auks.

As for Halyard, nothing affects him—except his involuntary seabath, and that did him so much good that he writes me from the South that he's going on a walking-tour through Switzerland—if I'll join him. I might have joined him if he had not married the pretty nurse. I wonder whether—But, of course, this is no place for speculation.

In regard to the harbor-master, you may believe it or not, as you choose. But if you hear of any great auks being found, kindly throw a table-cloth over their heads and notify the authorities at the new Zoological Gardens in Bronx Park, New York. The reward is ten thousand dollars.

Rats

M. R. James.

The sheer repulsiveness of the landscape where this story takes place is unique, and it is a pleasure to watch the hero and the villains romp across such a satisfying loathesome backdrop. I always find, several pages in, that I am beginning to smell the place.

"And if you was to walk through the bedrooms now, you'd see the ragged, moldy bedclothes a-heaving and a-heaving like seas." "And a-heaving and a-heaving with what?" he says. "Why, with the rats under 'em."

UT WAS it with the rats? I ask, because in another case it was not. I cannot put a date to the story, but I was young when I heard it, and the teller was old. It is an ill-proportioned tale, but that is my fault, not his.

It happened in Suffolk, near the coast. In a place where the road makes a sudden dip and then a sudden rise; as you go northward, at the top of that rise, stands a house on the left of the road. It is a tall red-brick house, narrow for its height; perhaps it was built about 1770. The top of the front has a low triangular pediment with a round window in the center. Behind it are stables and offices, and such garden as it has is behind them. Scraggy Scotch firs are near it: an expanse of gorse-covered land stretches away from it. It commands a view of the distant sea from the upper windows of the front. A sign on a post stands before the door; or did so stand, for though it was an inn of repute once, I believe it is so no longer.

To this inn came my acquaintance, Mr. Thomson, when he was a young man, on a fine spring day, coming from the University of Cambridge, and desirous of solitude in tolerable quarters and time for reading. These he found, for the landlord and his wife had been in service and could make a visitor comfortable, and there was no one else staying in the inn. He had a large room on the first floor commanding the road and the view, and if it faced east, why, that could not be helped; the house was well built and warm.

He spent very tranquil and uneventful days: work all the morning, an afternoon perambulation of the country round, a little conversation with country company or the people of the inn in the evening over the then fashionable drink of brandy and water, a little more reading and writing, and bed; and he would have been content that this should continue for the full month he had at disposal, so well was his work progressing, and so fine was the April of that year—which I have reason to believe was that which Orlando Whistlecraft chronicles in his weather record as the "Charming Year."

One of his walks took him along the northern road, which stands high and traverses a wide common, called a heath. On the bright afternoon when he first chose this direction his eye caught a white object some hundreds of yards to the left of the road, and he felt it necessary to make sure what this might be. It was not long before he was standing by it, and found himself looking at a square block of white stone fashioned somewhat like the base of a pillar, with a square hole in the upper surface. Just such another you may see at this day on Thetford Heath. After taking stock of it he contemplated for a few minutes the

view, which offered a church tower or two, some red
roofs of cottages and windows winking in the sun, and the
expanse of sea—also with an occasional wink and gleam
upon it—and so pursued his way.

In the desultory evening talk in the bar, he asked why
the white stone was there on the common.

"A old-fashioned thing, that is," said the landlord (Mr.
Betts), "we was none of us alive when that was put
there." "That's right," said another. "It stands pretty
high," said Mr. Thomson, "I dare say a sea-mark was on
it some time back." "Ah! yes," Mr. Betts agreed, "I 'ave
'eard they could see it from the boats; but whatever there
was, it's fell to bits this long time." "Good job too," said
a third, " 'twarn't a lucky mark, by what the old men
used to say; not lucky for the fishin', I mean to say."
"Why ever not?" said Thomson. "Well, I never see it myself," was the answer, "but they 'ad some funny ideas,
what I mean, peculiar, them old chaps, and I shouldn't
wonder but what they made away with it theirselves."

It was impossible to get anything clearer than this: the
company, never very voluble, fell silent, and when next
someone spoke it was of village affairs and crops. Mr.
Betts was the speaker.

Not every day did Thomson consult his health by taking a country walk. One very fine afternoon found him
busily writing at three o'clock. Then he stretched himself
and rose, and walked out of his room into the passage.
Facing him was another room, then the stair-head, then
two more rooms, one looking out to the back, the other to
the south. At the south end of the passage was a window,
to which he went, considering with himself that it was
rather a shame to waste such a fine afternoon. However,
work was paramount just at the moment; he thought he
would just take five minutes off and go back to it; and
those five minutes he would employ—the Bettses could
not possibly object—to looking at the other rooms in the
passage, which he had never seen. Nobody at all, it seemed,
was indoors; probably, as it was market day, they were

all gone to the town, except perhaps a maid in the bar. Very still the house was, and the sun shone really hot; early flies buzzed in the window-panes. So he explored. The room facing his own was undistinguished except for an old print of Bury St. Edmunds; the two next him on his side of the passage were gay and clean, with one window apiece, whereas he had two. Remained the southwest room, opposite to the last which he had entered. This was locked; but Thomson was in a mood of quite indefensible curiosity, and feeling confident that there could be no damaging secrets in a place so easily got at, he proceeded to fetch the key of his own room, and when that did not answer, to collect the keys of the other three. One of them fitted, and he opened the door. The room had two windows looking south and west, so it was as bright and the sun as hot upon it as could be. Here there was no carpet, but bare boards; no pictures, no washingstand, only a bed, in the farther corner: an iron bed, with mattress and bolster, covered with a bluish check counterpane. As featureless a room as you can well imagine, and yet there was something that made Thomson close the door very quickly and yet quietly behind him and lean against the windowsill in the passage, actually quivering all over. It was this, that under the counterpane someone lay, and not only lay, but stirred. That it was some *one* and not some *thing* was certain, because the shape of a head was unmistakable on the bolster; and yet it was all covered, and no one lies with covered head but a dead person; and this was not dead, not truly dead, for it heaved and shivered. If he had seen these things in dusk or by the light of a flickering candle, Thomson could have comforted himself and talked of fancy. On this bright day that was impossible. What was to be done? First, lock the door at all costs. Very gingerly he approached it and bending down listened, holding his breath; perhaps there might be a sound of heavy breathing, and a prosaic explanation. There was absolute silence. But as, with a rather tremulous hand, he put the key into its hole and

turned it, it rattled, and on the instant a stumbling pad-
ding tread was heard coming towards the door. Thomson
fled like a rabbit to his room and locked himself in: futile
enough, he knew it was; would doors and locks be any
obstacle to what he suspected? but it was all he could
think of at the moment, and in fact nothing happened;
only there was a time of acute suspense—followed by a
misery of doubt as to what to do. The impulse, of course,
was to slip away as soon as possible from a house which
contained such an inmate. But only the day before he had
said he should be staying for at least a week more, and
how if he changed plans could he avoid the suspicion of
having pried into places where he certainly had no
business? Moreover, either the Bettses knew all about the
inmate, and yet did not leave the house, or knew nothing,
which equally meant that there was nothing to be afraid
of, or knew just enough to make them shut up the room,
but not enough to weigh on their spirits: in any of these
cases it seemed that not much was to be feared, and certainly so far he had had no sort of ugly experience. On
the whole the line of least resistance was to stay.

Well, he stayed out his week. Nothing took him past
that door, and, often as he would pause in a quiet hour of
day or night in the passage and listen, and listen, no
sound whatever issued from that direction. You might
have thought that Thomson would have made some attempt at ferreting out stories connected with the inn—
hardly perhaps from Betts, but from the parson of the
parish, or old people in the village; but no, the reticence
which commonly falls on people who have had strange
experiences, and believe in them, was upon him. Nevertheless, as the end of his stay drew near, his yearning after some kind of explanation grew more and more acute.
On his solitary walks he persisted in planning out some
way, the least obtrusive, of getting another daylight
glimpse into that room, and eventually arrived at this
scheme. He would leave by an afternoon train—about
four o'clock. When his fly was waiting, and his luggage on

it, he would make one last expedition upstairs to look round his own room and see if anything was left unpacked, and then, with that key, which he had contrived to oil (as if that made any difference!), the door should once more be opened, for a moment, and shut.

So it worked out. The bill was paid, the consequent small talk gone through while the fly was loaded: "pleasant part of the country—been very comfortable, thanks to you and Mrs. Betts—hope to come back some time," on one side: on the other, "very glad you've found satisfaction, sir, done our best—always glad to 'ave your good word—very much favored we've been with the weather, to be sure." Then, "I'll just take a look upstairs in case I've left a book or something out—no, don't trouble, I'll be back in a minute." And as noiselessly as possible he stole to the door and opened it. The shattering of the illusion! He almost laughed aloud. Propped, or you might say sitting, on the edge of the bed was—nothing in the round world but a scarecrow! A scarecrow out of the garden, of course, dumped into the deserted room. . . . Yes; but here amusement ceased. Have scarecrows bare bony feet? Do their heads loll on to their shoulders? Have they iron collars and links of chain about their necks? Can they get up and move, if never so stiffly, across a floor, with wagging head and arms close at their sides? and shiver?

The slam of the door, the dash to the stair-head, the leap downstairs, were followed by a faint. Awaking, Thomson saw Betts standing over him with the brandy bottle and a very reproachful face. "You shouldn't a done so, sir, really you shouldn't. It ain't a kind way to act by persons as done the best they could for you." Thomson heard words of this kind, but what he said in reply he did not know. Mr. Betts, and perhaps even more Mrs. Betts, found it hard to accept his apologies and his assurances that he would say no word that could damage the good name of the house. However, they *were* accepted. Since the train could not now be caught, it was arranged that

Thomson should be driven to the town to sleep there. Before he went the Bettses told him what little they knew. "They says he was landlord 'ere a long time back, and was in with the 'ighwaymen that 'ad their beat about the 'eath. That's how he come by his end: 'ung in chains, they say, up where you see that stone what the gallus stood in. Yes, the fishermen made away with that, I believe, because they set it out at sea and it kep' the fish off, according to their idea. Yes, we 'ad the account from the people that 'ad the 'ouse before we come. 'You keep that room shut up,' they says, 'but don't move the bed out, and you'll find there won't be no trouble.' And no more there 'as been; not once he haven't come out into the 'ouse, though what he may do now there ain't no sayin'. Anyway, you're the first I know on that's seen him since we've been 'ere: I never set eyes on him myself, nor don't want. And ever since we've made the servants' rooms in the stablin' we ain't 'ad no difficulty that way. Only I do 'ope, sir, as you'll keep a close tongue, considerin' 'ow an 'ouse do get talked about": with more to this effect.

The promise of silence was kept for many years. The occasion of my hearing the story at last was this: that when Mr. Thomson came to stay with my father it fell to me to show him to his room, and instead of letting me open the door for him, he stepped forward and threw it open himself, and then for some moments stood in the doorway holding up his candle and looking narrowly into the interior. Then he seemed to recollect himself and said: "I beg your pardon. Very absurd, but I can't help doing that, for a particular reason." What that reason was I heard some days afterwards, and you have heard now.